CONFIDENCE 2

CONFIDENCE 2

MINDS SHINE BRIGHT

ANTHOLOGY 2024

Editor: Amanda Scotney
writing@mindsshinebright.com

Published by Minds Shine Bright in 2024
PO Box 1042
Windsor, 3181, VIC, Australia

Website: www.mindsshinebright.com
Subscribe: www.mindsshinebright.com/minds-shine-bright-blog
X: @msbwriting
Facebook: Minds Shine Bright | Melbourne VIC

Copyediting by Words Worthwhile
Proofreading by Millie Shilland
Book design and layout by Ampersand Duck
Cover artwork by Sharon McKenzie
Printed by IngramSpark

ISBN 978-0-6455231-4-0 (print)

A catalogue record for this book is available from the National Library of Australia

Minds Shine Bright acknowledges the people of the Kulin Nation, the Traditional Custodians of the land on which we live and work and where we have created this anthology. We pay respect to their long history and culture, and their Elders, past and present.

Special thanks to friends and family who have provided support and encouragement behind the scenes; and to the libraries, schools, organisations and groups that have helped writing and reading to flourish in safe havens; and to all those who have helped to promote the Minds Shine Bright writing competitions and anthologies. Thanks to all writers, poets and screenwriters who have submitted their work to Minds Shine Bright and thanks to all of our reviewers and readers.

This publication includes sensitive content, strong themes and language. Parental guidance is recommended for younger readers.

CONTENTS

INTRODUCTION

Welcome to the second anthology in our Confidence series. I'm really excited about launching and celebrating *Confidence 2 Minds Shine Bright Anthology 2024* online and at live events over the next few months.

Every anthology is a community, and working with and bringing parts of that community together gives me daily joy and inspiration. Being a micropublisher means there is much grunt work too, and growing our readership will be a key focus for the coming year.

This collection features forty-one winning and commended entries from the Minds Shine Bright international creative writing competition. It represents a continuation of our longitudinal exploration of the confidence theme in contemporary fiction and includes short stories, poems, flash fiction and a script.

Allow yourself to be carried away by a ragtag bunch of characters as they wander through the always open carnival of life. *Confidence 2* pulls together a reading experience that will break your heart open and then refill it to the brim with joy and wonder.

LOOKING BACK

Since late 2021, when Minds Shine Bright was formed, there has been a period of learning and growth. There are now over one hundred writers published in Minds Shine Bright anthologies, more than thirty-six thousand visitors have visited www.mindsshinebright.com; and we are slowly building connections with writers' groups, libraries, arts organisations, bookshops and readers.

The second Confidence writing competition ran from November 2022 to February 2023. During this time, the world's population exceeded eight billion;[1] inflation surged, contributing to a cost-of-living crisis;[2] natural disasters, including flooding, hurricanes and a devastating

---

[1]   United Nations, 'Population', Global Issues, UN website, n.d. https://www.un.org/en/global-issues/population, accessed 16 March 2024.

[2]   International Monetary Fund, 'Countering the cost-of-living crisis', World Economic Outlook Report, IMF website, 2022, https://www.imf.org/en/Publications/WEO/Issues/2022/10/11/world-economic-outlook-october-2022, accessed 16 March 2024.; and International Monetary Fund, 'Inflation peaking amid low growth', World Economic Outlook Report, IMF website, 2023 https://www.imf.org/en/Publications/WEO/Issues/2023/01/31/world-economic-outlook-update-january-2023, , accessed 16 March 2024.

earthquake in Turkey and Syria, wreaked destruction;[3] and the Ukraine–Russian war continued. In the United States, space flight to the moon resumed after fifty years and the James Webb Space Telescope captured images of distant galaxies from billions of years ago.[4] From a health perspective, life expectancy was lower during this period compared to pre-pandemic years.[5]

INTERPRETATIONS OF CONFIDENCE

Across all 590 entries, the most popular interpretations of the confidence theme explored 'relationships', 'self-confidence and resilience', followed closely by 'family tensions', 'animals and confidence', and 'youth and ageing'. There was a diverse range of relationship and dating stories, from awkward first dates to finding love and losing it. Many relationship stories took the reader on a path that often led to unexpected places.

Self-confidence and resilience writing was personal and powerful, recognising beauty as something that comes from within. Key interpretations of the theme were around learning and personal growth, persevering through difficult times, being yourself, and putting self-doubt and criticism into perspective.

While the top two topics were consistent with our earlier analysis (*Confidence 2022*), 'family tensions' was a surprise. Examples of this included tensions between parents, children and siblings; the pressure to meet expectations; the impacts of parenting young children—losing your sense of self and finding it again when you become an empty-nester; dispute resolutions; the impacts of addiction; and coping with cognitive decline. There was a small set of entries that delved into family violence and child exploitation. There were also entries about home and belonging—where mothers, fathers and grandparents were the subjects and confidence and family was explored in a tender, funny or joyous way.

[3]   F Urso, 'Natural disasters caused $313 bln economic losses in 2022—Aon', Reuters, 26 January 2023, https://www.reuters.com/business/environment/natural-disasters-caused-313-bln-economic-loss-2022-aon-2023-01-25/, accessed 16 March 2024.
[4]   NASA (www. Nasa.gov) 2022 in Review: Highlights from NASA in Silicon Valley, accessed 16 March 2024.
[5]   T Adair, H Houle and V Canudas-Romo, 'The rise and fall in Australia's life expectancy during the pandemic', Pursuit, 25 September 2023, https://pursuit.unimelb.edu.au/articles/the-rise-and-fall-in-australia-s-life-expectancy-during-the-pandemic, accessed 16 March 2024; and R H Shmerling, 'Why life expectancy in the US is falling', Harvard Health Publishing, 20 October 2022. https://www.health.harvard.edu/blog/why-life-expectancy-in-the-us-is-falling-202210202835.

Health and mental health were topics of great interest, and many writers examined confidence in hospital settings. The impact of social media and body image was closely related to reduced wellbeing by the writers, while accepting imperfection and nurturing strong self-esteem was linked to increased wellbeing. Dissatisfaction and lack of confidence were also topics of interest, as was loss.

Two emerging explorations were 'larger than life' and 'the outsider'. Sometimes 'the outsider' struggled to make connections and took us to darker places. At other times, 'the outsider' projected a sense of independence, strength, and freedom. 'Larger than life' entries entertained and captured something universal in a few words. Some of these pieces are joyous, celebrating life and love, and some capture cyclical elements: the sun, the Ferris wheel, the City Circle tram and the rising escalator.

Nature continued to be a source of inspiration and replenishment, but also a source of danger. The arts and the creative writing process continued to provide food for thought, and inspiration. Women, gender, and identity continued to be popular choices, and there was an interesting contrast between entries that explored team spirit and those that focused on office politics. Once again, the confidence trickster rose as the bad guy, breaking the rules and sometimes coming undone.

The analysis of themes across the entries was done after *Confidence 2* had been curated and the winner had been announced, enabling the winning and commended entries to tell their own story.

In curating *Confidence 2* the forty-one entries formed a story that builds layers of experience, feeling and meaning to create a narrative curve similar to a novel. The anthology starts by exploring nature and our place in it and then moves on to examine and celebrate life and the universal. Next, human vulnerabilities and strengths are explored through experiences with health and the health system. A range of stories and poems about gender looks at the things that bring us together and the things that drive us apart. The narrative returns to nature to examine how water can lull us into a state of inner luminescence, shift and change our moods and throw us around. In 'Reflections and Paths to Healing', nature and art provide moments of nadir or epiphany, and each character is on an inner journey that could lead to loss of self or healing. In 'The Outsider' a motley bunch of characters tell stories of vulnerability and strength, grief, humour, loneliness, despair, and the power of hope. In 'Subconscious Explorations' new horizons are explored and boundaries are questioned.

There was a range of writing styles submitted from classical forms to newer forms such as prose poetry and experimental fiction. The script selected was a stage play (in 2022 Jed Stanley's screenplay *Beaucoup Bills* won the category prize).

In bringing works together from different countries there was a need to balance the unique features of the language and grammar with having a cohesive Minds Shine Bright style. To preserve the integrity of each piece you will find both Australian/British and American conventions included.

ABOUT THE EDITOR

Amanda Scotney is a writer, poet, independent filmmaker and the Founder of Minds Shine Bright. She was born in Hobart, Tasmania, and currently resides in Melbourne, Victoria, Australia. Amanda is passionate about promoting the arts and is the judge of the Minds Shine Bright writing competition. She also enjoys travelling and discovering beauty in natural settings.

ABOUT MINDS SHINE BRIGHT

Minds Shine Bright is an arts organisation committed to supporting writers and encouraging communities of readers and writers to come together and spread the love of anthologies.

The Minds Shine Bright writing competition is run annually from August to April. The Confidence writing competition alternates with a Seasons writing competition, which has a theme based on the external environment. The third Minds Shine Bright Confidence writing competition is scheduled to open in August 2024 and will run until April 2025.

Minds Shine Bright anthologies are available at the online Minds Shine Bright Bookshop and in bookshops and libraries. In addition to *Confidence 2*, our titles include the original *Confidence* anthology, our first publication, created during the topsy-turvy early days of the COVID-19 pandemic, as well as the Seasons anthologies. *Storm* features the storm-inspired work of twenty-eight writers and poets. *Light and Shadow*, the second Seasons anthology, is currently in development.

THE WINNING ENTRIES

The forty writers published in this anthology are representative of a wider group of writers exploring the confidence theme. In February 2024, they gathered online to read and share their stories and poems, and the winners were announced.

Each winner is listed below with a sentence or two about what stood out in the judging process and some words from the writers about what inspired their winning piece.

FIRST PRIZE

The First Prize was awarded to Helen Booth from Anglesea, Victoria, Australia, for her short story *Drift*.

Drift stood out because it was engaging on many levels. It captures an authentic feeling of life on a farm, the wild and dangerous beauty of the mountains, and the energy and connections between a group of young friends, seeking distractions and risk, at the cusp of their adult lives.

The first spark for Drift *was a story a friend told me about his son rescuing a skier from a tree well. At the time, I was tutoring several young men in VCE English. They all excelled at sport, maths and science but struggled with English.* Drift *began as a story about procrastination in the face of that struggle, but throughout the rewriting process, as different parts of the story began speaking to each other, it took deeper meaning.*   Helen Booth

POETRY PRIZE

The Poetry Prize was awarded to Valerie Wallace from Michigan City, Indiana, for her poem *Carnelevarium*.

Carnelevarium is a celebration of the human body, its cells, connections and twinkling life force, through the metaphor of a carnival. The rhythm and structure of the last stanza creates the sensation of a merry-go-round or Ferris wheel slowly gaining momentum.

I wrote the first line of this poem on a dreary day and realized I wanted to make a poem that would capture how, even in times of distress, or when lacking ability or confidence in the world, there is always this gift of our body. I wanted to focus on the body's inner workings—its pizazz and delight, how there is this container of joyful energy we walk around with.
Valerie Wallace

The Short Story Prize was awarded to Dan Micklethwaite from Yorkshire, United Kingdom, for his story *Blackpool Solo.*

Blackpool Solo stood out because of its clarity of expression. It explored some of the darker and more fragile moments of a character who had lost hope (or had he?) and the importance of human connection.

The seed of this story was planted while approaching the eponymous seaside town, when I noticed the bizarre, almost mocking, similarity between a telecoms mast and the old Tower in the distance. Over time, it made me think of the way that external projections can distort and erode our sense of self-worth, if we let them, and how that can take us down a path from which it's difficult to return. The character of Julian, with his frustrated ambitions, developed naturally from there.   Dan Micklethwaite

FLASH FICTION PRIZE

The Flash Fiction Prize was awarded to Kathryn Le Mon from Columbus, Ohio, for *When I Am the Wolf.*

When I Am the Wolf takes the metaphor of a wolf to new places and celebrates the confidence, strength and creativity of a young woman. The wolf seems to be alive as the crowd in the stadium cheers.

This story was inspired by the Little Red Riding Hood fairy tale. I wondered what I could create if I made this little girl become the wolf through a school-mascot costume, and I discovered a story about the different ways of owning one's girlhood and adolescence through performance and make-believe.   Kathryn Le Mon

SCRIPT PRIZE

The Script Prize was awarded to Grace Keller from Dallas, Texas, for *The Last Ten Seconds.*

The *Last Ten Seconds* stood out because of the character development and the feisty voice of the main character, Lila, as she meets three other versions of herself from different stages of her life. It examines how life experiences and the choices we make can change us and increase or diminish our capacity to live life to the full.

My inspiration was thinking about what really happens in the last ten seconds of your life. People always say that your life flashes before your eyes right before you die. That, for me, always seemed really intense. I started thinking about a way that time would slow down and you'd really be able to take in your life. I was also interested in pocket dimensions. A pocket dimension is a small area outside of our universe that has a different time/ space rhythm. A character can take as much time as they need while not using up their time in our world. And from those thoughts, The Last Ten Seconds *was born.* Grace Keller

IN NATURE

DRAWING ON NATURE

MOLLY DUNN　BOOROLITE, VIC, AUS

Here stands crippled cluster of trees, head bent
From rain drumming black, from passing clouds grey
Weary and whipped, alone in their way
Among which secrets hover, reticent
Tales but a flicker—discordant lament
Rebirth of those dead-eyed, cloaked in regrets
Of dreams tossed aside, ambition they let
Be smothered by streets of crawling cement.
Yet here, the inevitability
Of slow death by civility, is made
Baseless, compared to the gentle wonder
Of beauty found limning the twisted boughs
Muddied wallaby tracks, eddies of shade
That offer life beyond life; offer breath.

DRIFT

HELEN BOOTH   ANGLESEA, VIC, AUS

His father's face, dream words merging with magpie calls, the soft tap of spoons on breakfast bowls, the smell of toast. Jake opens his eyes to the grey outlines of his bedroom and throws back the doona. Shit. Why didn't they wake him? Surely they wouldn't go without him. Then the jolt of last night. In the yellow light of the shed, his father pressing a bundle of folded towels into his chest saying, 'Put those in the bag, mate.' His mother at the bench lining up plastic sleeves, iodine, gloves, scissors. Him asking her, 'What time are we going?' Her asking him, 'Have you done those essays?' 'Nah. Nah.' Him laughing and pushing the towels into the bag. 'They're only practice essays. Not worth anything.' 'Well, you're not going anywhere till they're done.' Him laughing again. 'Come on, Mum.' 'No,' she says. 'No.' He looks at his father. His father shakes his head. 'You heard your mother. You're barely scraping through. Remember? No English, no Ag College.'

Jake sits on the edge of his bed, shivering, wondering if he should go down the hall to see them off. Fuck 'em. No. Why should he? He crawls back into the fug of his bed. Rolls over to face the wall. They'd regret it when they got out there; ewes in trouble, lambs orphaned and only two pairs of hands. He closes his mind to their footsteps, the bang of the door, the gurgle of diesel as the old farm ute bursts to life, revving and grunting through gears and trailing off along the track to the paddocks.

Cold silence greets him when he wakes hours later. He picks up his clothes from the floor, takes them to the loungeroom and dresses by the log fire his father stoked earlier.

Starving, he hovers at the open fridge door. Peels cling wrap from a plate. Slips his hand under the last quarter of apple pie his mother baked yesterday and takes large bites. Crumbs of buttery pastry scatter across the front of his jumper and fall to the floor. He washes it down with orange juice and throws the empty bottle onto the bench. Then he searches the fridge for margarine and jam and nudges the door shut, leaving the empty pie plate and curling cling wrap on the shelf.

Sated on toast, he drifts to his room, turns his laptop on, lines up his notebook, the text, biros, highlighters and sticky notes, all the while picturing his parents struggling to cope without him. He pulls up the blind to lemony winter sunshine. Such a waste being stuck inside, a day of study stretching out like a never-ending yawn.

He flicks through the pages of *The Women of Troy*. Such a skinny book. When he picked it up from the second-hand bookshop last summer, he thought it would be a cinch. *Wrong*. Too many characters with strange names speaking streams of words he can't understand. The play only made sense when his teacher explained it. Later, when he tries to analyse prompts and figure out a response, he gets nowhere. It sends him into a panic, like that time a few years ago when he'd wandered into the bush, turned around and lost all sense of direction. Gum trees and scrub crowded in on him, hiding any route back to his family, who were sitting on the riverbank waiting for fish to bite. He'd spun in circles. Hot. Dizzy. Searching for his footprints and broken twigs. Only his father's echoing cheers and laughter showed him the way. His dad reeling in a trout while Jake stood in the bush shitting himself.

He always tops the class in maths, chem, and physics. Now, a slow pulse of failure creeps through him, throbbing inside his head and settling behind his eyes. He grabs his phone, long fingers curving around its light weight. If he looked at it, the day would be gone. Lost in funny dances and the lure of beautiful girls who live and breathe TikTok.

Ping.

He turns the phone over and traces his passcode. Of course, it's Marco.

snow!!!?

Typical. He's not studying. English never bothers him. He just copies his cousin Rosie's essays from last year. Memorises them for the exams. He'll be fine. His future sealed at the family vineyard—picking, pruning, packing, serving at the restaurant and cellar door.

Jake stabs his thumbs at the keyboard: can't (three frowning faces) English essays (three vomiting faces)

Ping: i'll send you rosie's

Jake sends a laughing face and six birds.

Marco, persistent, as usual.

2 hours tops

Jake fires back: not today talk 2 u later

Silence. A blank Word document glares at him from his laptop. Blank, except for the nagging pulse of the cursor. Like a foot tapping or a hand drumming fingers on his desk, waiting for his words. Waiting for his words to add up to sentences and paragraphs of meaning. Jake craves something to help him concentrate—hot chocolate or coffee with heaps of sugar. He wanders back to the kitchen and flicks on the kettle.

Ping.

Marco, again.

Jake eyes his father's keys lying on the bench. Since getting his licence, whenever Jake borrows the car, Marco rides shotgun. For years, they'd ridden around the valley on their bikes and bumped along together on the back seat of the school bus. Now, as designated passenger, Marco navigates adventures across wider terrain.

The kettle boils and steams while Jake leans on the bench, reading Marco's text: cait's coming

Caitlin. The third amigo. Nice move, Marco.

Heat blows through the vents. Marco wriggles in his seatbelt, trying to remove his puffer jacket. 'Just undo it.' Caitlin laughs from the back. 'Undo the seatbelt. Take your jacket off. Put the belt on again.' Jake snatches glimpses of her in the rear-view mirror. Sunlight plays through streaks of gold in her hair. He takes a bend a little too fast, and she yells, 'Hey, slow down.' He hits the brakes, skidding on gravel, her hair flying. He corrects and bounces back onto bitumen. Marco lurches from side to side. 'Really? You want me to take the seatbelt off with him at the wheel?'

Ice on the road ahead. Jake slows. Concentrates. Grips the steering wheel, willing the tyres to likewise grip bitumen. He can't be bothered stopping to put chains on. To his left is a steep drop; tall trees sprinkled with snow, marching down to the valley. To his right, patches of snow lie over boulders and leaf litter at the base of massive, gnarled trees, and the mountain rises, rocky, heavily treed and becoming whiter with each bend. The sun brightens, lighting blue sky and a glare of snow. Jake reaches into the consul for his sunglasses.

'I like the look,' Marco says. He's finally managed to drag his jacket off and is rolling and unrolling it in his lap. That's Marco. Never still. Especially on the footy field, where he darts and ducks, throwing himself at the ball and his opponents without a thought. He plays crazy hard. Never gives up. But with his extra height, Jake is the winner, the hero who leaps into the air, snatches the ball and sends it hurtling between the big white posts.

Marco searches through his jacket pockets for his sunglasses. 'Ah, there you are.' He pulls down the visor, slides the mirror open, ceremoniously slips on his aviators and turns his head this way and that.

'I like mine better,' he says, running fingers through dark hair, twisting in his seat to show Caitlin. 'What do ya think?' Her silvery laughter fills the car. 'Yeah, too good. Like a real celeb.' She leans forward, and Marco snaps a couple of selfies with her.

Jake strains to keep his eyes on the road. Each bend winds into the next, snow piling along both sides. 'Should've brought the skis,' Marco says. Jake shakes his head. Marco punches Jake's leg. 'Should've taken Rosie's essays—they'd never know. I used the one on futility of war.' He announces 'futility of war' with a flourish, like he's an expert. 'Ten years of war all because some dude's wife ran away to marry another dude.' Caitlin says nothing. Jake wonders what she thinks of Marco's cheating and what she might think if he did it. Time's running out. Maybe it's his only option—change a few words, shift some paragraphs. 'Here it comes, Jakey-boy,' Marco says. 'Next left.'

The day visitor car park sits on the first plateau, where cross-country trails snake through the forest and across little bridges over creeks bubbling with melted snow. Jake takes the turn smoothly, tyres crunching, wheels rolling to a halt. Apart from them, the car park is empty. Jake glances in the rear-view mirror. Caitlin pulling on her beanie. How perfect is her olive skin? Every pore smooth, glowing. He watches her zipping her jacket, slipping on gloves. Yesterday they'd worked the same shift at the General Store. Standing side by side, stacking shelves with tins of baked beans and soup, reaching into a box, their hands sometimes touching.

Marco escapes the car before them, pacing, ready to go. 'C'mon, guys. What are you waiting for?' He runs to the start of the track. Scoops up a handful of snow, slaps it into a ball and hurls it at the car. 'C'mon.' The snowball thwacks and splatters against Jake's window. Caitlin slams her door and stands on the other side, arms out, breathing deeply, exhaling puffs of white condensation. Choo-choo trains. They'd played that game when they were kids. He remembers her little face and those yellow bumblebee gumboots she always wore, even in summer. How would they play that game now—her mouth open, lips soft and pink, eyes focused on misty clouds of breath? He leans back and watches.

Thwack. A snowball hits the windscreen. Jake gathers himself, his jacket, gloves, keys. Checks the ignition—off. Gearstick—in park. Handbrake—on. Marco appears at the window, opens the door and drags Jake out. 'Mate, what are you doing? C'mon.'

Jake pushes the lock button on his father's keys. Cold air stings his face. He tosses his gloves and the keys on the bonnet and fights with the sleeves of his jacket. Hands icy-cold, he zips up, drives his hands into his gloves and wanders around to join Caitlin in the choo-choo-train game. But that moment's gone. He follows her gaze across the plateau and down slopes and gullies draped in folds of snow. 'Wish we could ski,' she says. 'Yeah. I know. I've got those practice essays.' Jake bends down, picks up a handful of snow, runs his fingers through it and watches the icy crumbs drizzle to the ground. 'Have you started?' she asks. Jake grins and shakes his head. 'Nah. You?'

'Yeah. I'm done.' Of course, she is. Caitlin's up at five every morning mucking out horse shelters and riding her pony. She plans ahead, chips away at every task. If anything stumps her, she emails the teacher. He never needs help with his other subjects and won't ask for it in English. 'Have you chosen prompts? Worked out contentions and plans?' He laughs. 'Nah… I… that book… it just doesn't make sense.' She nudges him hard, and he lurches sideways. Takes a step to stay upright. 'Should've told me,' she says, hooking her arm through his. He drifts down the track, beside her, carried on the lilt of her voice, the rise and fall of her insights and emphasis. Telling him how Hecuba, her daughters and the other women keep their dignity after suffering violence, rape and massive losses at the hands of Menelaus and his soldiers. Irony—only the audience and Cassandra (*which one is she?*) know that the gods will punish them. In the end, no one wins.

Jake stops. Looks to the sky, then at Caitlin. 'Yeah, but he got his ex-wife back.' Caitlin turns on him, eyes wide. 'Only after he totally destroys a beautiful city, murders Hecuba's husband and every other male—even babies—and divvies the women up between his mates as personal slaves. What kind of man does that?'

Wow. This is real for her. Not just some old story. She's fired up, like his mum gets when the TV splashes news of women raped or murdered and kids killed and his mum yells at the TV, 'Another one. Another bloody man who can't take no for an answer.'

Now it made sense. 'So… innocent women and children suffer because Menelaus can't handle it when Helen leaves.' Caitlin nods. 'Yeah. Everyone suffers for his revenge. His pride. Even his own soldiers. Like Marco said, futile.'

Like Marco said? Jake sinks his boot into the trail and kicks up a spray of snow. Marco knew jack shit.

'Hey, you two. Wait up.' Jake turns, his arm still linked with Caitlin's.

Marco kneels in the snow a few metres behind, doing up his shoelace, his hair falling across shiny aviators. He stands, pushes back his hair and grins. 'You know, Jakey-boy, you should be more careful.' He raises his hand in the air and dangles something that glints in the sunshine.

Jake squints. Pats his pockets. His dad's Bomber's key tag spins on the end of the chain hanging from Marco's fingers. Shit. He'd almost lost the keys.

'Aren't you gonna say thank you?' Marco's tone is strange… Sneering. Bitter. It sticks in Jake's throat. He cannot swallow it. Cannot form words. 'Why, you're welcome,' Marco says, throwing the keys high in the air.

Jake stretches his right arm. Splays his fingers. Leaps at the keys. Doesn't even get a touch. The keys sail through the air and plummet somewhere on the other side of the track.

'Oh, mate, you can do better than that. Must be losing your touch.'

What is this… this baiting thing Marco's doing? Caitlin's arm presses against his as they stand, scanning the snow. No keys. Here he is again. In that forest. Lost. The sweat of trouble builds inside him, across his chest, up his neck and face. Marco pushes between them. Hands on his hips. 'Should've caught 'em, mate.' He laughs. Jake's jaw clenches. His cheek pulses. 'What the fuck, Marco?' He slams Marco in the chest. Marco falls backwards, legs out, hands breaking his fall. 'Oh, so that's how it is?' Instead of retaliating, Marco scrambles to his feet and storms up the track towards the car.

Caitlin stays beside Jake. 'See anything?' he asks. She doesn't reply. Her eyes aren't even on the snow; they're on Marco, following him as he trudges up the track. 'Oh. Sorry.' She returns her gaze to the slope. 'No… nothing… What if we can't find them?'

Good question. He'd have to call his father. Interrupt the lambing. Get him to drive the old ute all the way here with the spare key. Jake burns with the consequences, eyes darting across the snow between and under trees where he thinks the keys landed, but there's a lot of snow and everything looks the same until… 'There. Over there.' He points at a flash of silver and Bomber's red.

Jake stares at that gleam of red below as he removes his gloves and thrusts them at Caitlin. He notes the tree, the direction and the short slope leading down to the tree before he climbs over large rocks edging the track.

Unlike the track, the snow on the other side is soft and covers his boots. He takes small steps forward. Freezing air thick with scents of peppery leaves and wet bark burns the insides of his nostrils. He bends his knees, leans back, treads the slope as lightly as possible, sinking calf-deep with every step. This is why people wear skis. This is why the signs tell you to stick to the trails. The keys lie in a slight hollow under the canopy of a tree. He steps through, beneath the canopy, grabs a rough, low-angled branch with his left hand, steps forward, bends and sweeps the keys up with his right hand. 'Yay!' Caitlin whoops, whistles, and claps. For a moment he's lit with the double triumph of her cheers and the keys in his hand. Seconds later, the snow beneath his feet crumbles and he shoots down. Engulfed. Covered. Packed in, except for the dragging strain on his armpit and the prickle of bark in his left hand as he clings to the branch.

Cold. Cold face. Freezing. Burning cold all over. Dark. Sunglasses squashed against his face. Right arm wedged to his side. Air. Short breaths. Panting. Fuck, fuck, fuck. Thudding heart. Muffled screams above. Relax. Try not to move. Remember that guy who fell into the silo and drowned in a sea of grain? Snow isn't grain. Doesn't move like grain. He'll be okay. Marco and Caitlin will get help. No. There's no signal. And no keys to drive for help. The keys. Where are they? Lost. From above comes a regular muted sound. A voice. Calm. Repetitious. 'Da da da da. Da daa da da da da da daa.' On it goes. Over and over.

How can they get him out without falling in themselves? He is gonna die down here, for sure. Suffocate or freeze to death. Faced with death, he expects his life to flash before him. But it doesn't. Instead something bitter and metallic slices through him, a taste of those ancient Greek soldiers. Inside of him. That piece of him that's got to be king of the school, king of the girls, king of the footy. That piece that battles against the world whenever he's not winning. What's the word for that? Selfish… arrogant… No. That word his mum uses… he can't remember. Tears warm his face. His mind races, searching for his mother's word. Searching for that value, the answer to that equation. Words—answers—symbols for feelings. Like letters in algebra waiting for you to discover and number, the value. Like that muffled song from above, 'Da da da da. Da daa da da da da da daa.' No words, but feelings that hint at the value and meaning of those sounds— *soothing, encouraging.* He's getting to the answer. Feelings—like letters in algebra—added to, subtracted, multiplied or divided by decisions, choices, actions, reactions. Finding words, understanding symbols, putting words together, understanding and solving complex problems, multi-dimensional equations. No single answer. Infinite combinations, infinite permutations, infinite possible results, depending on whatever operations people choose to apply. Then he remembers that word his father made up to describe certain politicians—*deludicrous*. And he's laughing through tears and wishing his father were here now, back from the lambing and able to drag him out.

His arm and fingers ache from the cold and the strain of hanging on. Unlike a lamb presenting with one foot out, he must leave his hand out there. He wriggles his toes. Flexes his feet. What is that he's standing on? Something hard. Maybe a boulder in a rocky outcrop buried beneath snow. He slides his feet. Tiny sideways movements. Finds the edges. No. Too narrow. Not rock. A branch. The branch under his feet and the branch he's holding onto with his left hand are part of the same tree. A large tree, buried under metres of snow. If he lets go, if he slips, he'll never get out.

Bit by bit, he slides his feet sideways towards the trunk, clinging to the branch above. He balances, one foot in front of the other, and twists his body repeatedly, displacing snow and turning to face the trunk. As he inches towards the trunk, the drag on his left arm eases. Almost there, till a jolt shoots through his guts and pierces his chest as his right foot slips from the branch and sinks into snow. He kicks out. Left knee bending. Weight tugging at his armpit. Bark tearing at his fingers as his grip on the branch above loosens. Someone grabs his wrist, holds his arm tight. He kicks again. Drags his foot up. Secures it on the branch.

Legs shaking, he edges his feet along the branch until his nose and right shoulder crunch against bark. He holds tight with his left hand and slides his right hand up the trunk and punches at the snow above his head. Straining and puffing, he punches up, again and again. Each punch dents and thins the ceiling of snow. Each punch brings Caitlin's voice closer, till at last he puts singsong words to feelings, 'It's okay, Jake. We're here, and we're getting you out. It's okay, Jake. We're here, and we're getting you out.'

Please. Don't let her fall in.

One more punch, and his fist breaks through, fingers sprouting like seedlings. He reaches up. Something soft. Caitlin's hair. Caitlin's wet gloves wrapping around his hand. He pushes beyond, reaching up to meet his other hand, grabbing the branch in the fork where it meets the trunk. Two arms out. Head in position. Feet raise, one by one. Knees bent, he pushes against the trunk like a lamb ready to enter the world. With all the power in his shoulders and arms, he drags himself up.

His head bursts through. Air. Space. So much air. So much space. Panting. Breathing. Alive.

'Oh, Jake. There you are.' Caitlin's lying on her stomach, away from the hole, on the other side of the tree. She brushes snow from his hair and cheeks. Tries to straighten his sunglasses. 'Hmmm. They're a little crooked.' She's smiling, but tears trickle down her face and over that fine pale ridge that traces the outline of her top lip.

'Oh, God. Thank you. Thank you, Cait. I thought I was a goner.'

'You're not out yet, dickhead.'

Marco. Jake strains his neck. Marco's kneeling behind Caitlin, holding her legs while Jake feels the weight of her hands scraping snow from his neck and shoulders as he clings to the tree like a monkey, hands gripping the branch above, legs still buried and wrapped around the trunk. 'Watch out, Cait. I'm climbing out.'

She shimmies backwards.

Jake unwraps his legs, pushes his feet against the trunk, knees bent. With one hand, he reaches and grabs the next branch up and steps up the trunk, displacing more snow. Hand after hand. Foot after foot. He sheds snow and climbs out, hauling himself onto a thick branch where he sits, legs dangling and breathing hard. His broken sunglasses fall off and tumble into the hole, joining the lost keys. His blood rushes in his ears as he takes in wide blue sky and vast white slopes. He's done it. He's got himself out.

'You gonna sit up there all day, stupid?'

Jake laughs. 'Good to see you making yourself useful, idiot.' They were back, him and Marco, their rough words symbols of care. 'I'm coming down,' says Jake, wrapping his arms around the trunk, swinging himself around to the side away from the hole. Bark gouges his hands as he steps and slides down the tree, hanging for a moment before letting go. Rolling onto the snow and lying on his stomach beside Caitlin.

'You okay?' she asks. 'Yeah… feels weird. Really good, but weird. Like I've been to another planet. Everything looks clearer, brighter… kind of more real than before.' Jake props on his elbows, breathes in chilly air and sighs. 'Look at you.' Caitlin smiles. 'Choo-choo trains.' Jake throws his arm over her shoulder and hugs her. 'You remember, huh? When we were little…'

'Hey, you two. Can't hang around like this all day,' Marco yells. Caitlin squeals and slides away as Marco drags her by her ankles to the safety of the track. 'You're next, Jakey-boy. Don't move.' Maybe Marco likes her. Maybe she likes Marco. Jake would ask her. Find the words. Tell her how he feels. Be ready to accept whatever she might say.

The surge of adrenaline slows, cooling his body to constant shivers. Drenched jeans cling to his legs. His hands sting from cuts and scratches. Drops of bright blood stain the snow. Something hard bites into his thigh. He slides his hand under his leg, feels flat snow beneath his palm and something jagged rubbing against knuckles. Something deep inside his pocket. Lumpy, rounded with hard, sharp, offshoots—the keys. His father's keys! Must have shoved them in his pocket moments before the snow caved in. He can't wait to tell the others. Like some weird snow angel, he lays on his stomach and manoeuvres his body around to face the direction of the track. He gets into a low crawl and gradually propels himself up the slope to level ground.

'Hey, thought I told you not to move,' Marco yells. 'You think Cait's gonna dig you out again?'

Jake stops, sits up, leans back on one elbow and pulls the keys from his pocket. 'Look. Look what I've got.' He laughs. He holds up the keys, the silver chain and Bomber's tag twirling in the air. Caitlin whistles and cheers. 'Yes! So glad we don't have to walk home.' Marco puts his head in his hands. 'Geez, mate… I never meant to… You could have…'

Jake laughs. 'It's okay. It doesn't matter… I got 'em. I got the keys, and I got out.'

'Let's go, then,' Marco says. He and Caitlin are about eight metres away. They tread lightly towards him. Marco wraps his hands around one of Jake's ankles, Cait takes the other and they run, dragging him in. Jake collapses onto his back, clutching the keys, sliding across powdery snow. The three of them laugh, screaming and falling about in that *loud-crazy-out-of-control-can't-stop-laughing-over-the-top-best-ever-happy-kind-of-way.*

JUDGEMENT DAY

F.L. ROSE   BURRAGATE, NSW, AUS

You forgot.

You took the dogs to the dam, the housemate and you. All three of them; his slug-bodied pug cross with the permanent fungal infection, the happy-family-advert beagle, and your sharp-muzzled kelpie. He—the housemate—was not one for swimming in dams, or even walking to them. He liked the clean chlorinated clarity of the local pool, with its carefully monitored bacterial count. But it was a hot day, and the pool was a long drive, and the dogs were eager, and you said, 'Why don't we take them for a dip?'

And he said, 'Okay.'

You stepped through the grass, cut short in places so you could scour for snakes, those shining slivers of black disappearing from under your feet. The dogs jumped over them, without seeing, as a slim tail whisked into the grass. The housemate took off his T-shirt, which had the name of some football team blazoned on it, and hung it on a black wattle branch. The housemate's tanned, avocado-shaped torso caught the dappled light of the water above his surfer shorts.

You said, 'Watch them go!' and threw a stick into the dam.

The little pug trundled out like a tugboat, short front legs pedalling, back legs struggling to keep up, tail like a rudder. But the kelpie leapt out like an Olympic swimmer off the blocks, dark and swift and single-minded. She reached the stick first and forged back in triumph through the clear silvered water. You felt sorry for the slug-dog. He tried.

'Here,' the housemate said, and tossed a ball, a consolation prize for the little one. It was no good; the kelpie dropped the stick and got that too.

Meanwhile, the beagle waited in the longer grass, with his magisterial tea-coloured eyes following every move.

It was hot. The housemate wasn't looking. You took off your shirt and pants and waded in through the muddied shallows. There's always that first shock of cool, but only for a second, then you were dog-paddling out to the centre, the beagle following. Deep green beneath, cloudless above, you swam through the reflections of the trees, amid dragonflies and skaters and tea-tree blossom. Safe in the water, you called to the housemate, 'You coming in?'

So *he* waded in with his big, soft feet, the dogs eddying around him like children. He was a good swimmer, the housemate, but frightened of things he couldn't see underneath. You might have told him that they're more likely to be waiting in the shallows, among the mud and reeds, than in the deep centre, but you didn't. Funny how such a big man could be so timid, you thought, revelling in your own bush toughness.

You forgot about it. In the embrace of nature, you forgot that you were sixty yesterday, that your bottom hangs out of your pants and your breasts stretch your black bra top southwards, especially when it's wet. You forgot that your stomach isn't flat anymore and that your arms aren't taut and that there are age spots all over your back and veins on your legs. You forgot that you weren't young because, in this place, you were.

The housemate got anxious. 'Snuffles!' he called to his dog, 'Snuffles, come in now, come on, get on out!'

With his little legs circling, Snuffles beat the water aside, like a tiny fat crocodile, and snorted as he carried yet another piece of dam weed to the shore. He wasn't tired, not him. But the housemate became more insistent.

'He starts to sink after a while,' he explained, waist deep, fussing from the shallows. 'He needs to rest.'

Well, if he does sink, you thought, nobody will find him. It was deep, this dam, twenty feet or more. You could picture the squat body of the dog spiralling down like a plug. Still, in your experience, dogs don't.

Cattle dogs, you knew about, and border collies, and mutts. You couldn't sink them if you tried. But Snuffles was different. When you looked back at him, you could see all the buoyancy was in the front of him, while the smaller back end was indeed beginning to sag downwards. Like yours.

You shoved the dog towards the shore with a hand on his curly-tailed rear, chucking the dam weed after him as encouragement. The housemate called him close. Then he waded out, dried himself proudly on the bank, stretched, a man in his prime.

But you and the kelpie kept swimming, swimming. You had had enough; it was time to go in now, go up to the house and get coffee— you could feel your innards tighten with morning hunger—but you didn't want to come out.

Because you forgot.

You forgot that you didn't shave your bikini line this week—haven't done it for months. You forgot the way your stomach droops like a half-filled balloon over the top of your wet undies, and all the hair on your body snakes downwards like threadworms. You forgot that you were sixty yesterday. You should have worn something more concealing. You forgot because, well, generally you swim naked in the dam when no one is there, and they mostly aren't—it's just you and the birds. You forgot because you don't look in mirrors anymore.

And then—when the housemate displayed himself—you remembered all those things. And there he was sitting on the bank, waiting, with his two dogs staring out at you beside him, and you just knew that he'd see all the things you'd rather no one did, though he would pretend not to— he was a decent man, the housemate. You imagined him saying to his girlfriend later, 'You don't want to see what I saw the other day. An old woman getting out of the dam in her bikini—not a pretty sight, I can tell you!' And she, being lean and fortyish, might quickly run her hand over her flat, hard stomach and think, 'I'm not there yet, thank God.'

Round and round, the kelpie circled like a shark while you put off the inevitable. The housemate said,

'I think I'll go up now and put the kettle on.'

You waved at him, submersed. 'Sure, sounds good.' You do that, you thought, relieved. Off you go, and away.

But the two little dogs, the pug and the beagle, decided to stay and stare. As if they were waiting on you, a Miss Universe panel determined to judge your exit, whether you liked it or not. And since they weren't going, he stayed too. If he hadn't been a man, he could have been a hen sitting on eggs.

You made a decision. You swept in towards the edge with your strong old arms; you reached the shallows; you stood up, the shining wet falling from your shoulders like a veil. Let him see, let him judge, you thought recklessly. You were sixty yesterday, what do you care?

You put your shirt back on, your pants, shook out your hair, and started back up to the house, kelpie smiling at your side.

Yes, why should you care? And—you realised, all wet and glad, with the grass flicking your shins—you really didn't.

LARGER THAN LIFE

CARNELEVARIUM

VALERIE WALLACE   MICHIGAN CITY, INDIANA, US

Do me this favor, and love your body
by which I mean, your heart's lightning, beguiling
lymph, that heavy brain of yours, spine and all.

What helps us reach for another? hums my body
to yours, electric pulse & disturb sparkling inside us both.
We crack and quiver all by ourselves.
Our minutes blur by, sweet and noxious,
cells performing their rites, winking without stop.

We heave for the prize
but what merriment, that daily we pour water
into ourselves and squirt out something altogether different!

From one carnival to another, I beg you indulge
in the sticky gore, the thrilling dismount, your breath's susurration.
Your ticket may be a fancy eyebrow,
spit, sphincter, a spot neglected,
your skin's dimensionality, waving attention

to its wheel of you. How each time you move, the world
changes, around and again the lights slip on,
the ecstatic buzz already begun.

WHEN I AM THE WOLF

KATHRYN LE MON   COLUMBUS, OHIO, US

Beneath the bleachers is another kind of belly, dark and roiling with noise: the fans and onlookers pound their feet in ceremonial exuberance, and I emerge into the gymnasium as a second birth. The fluorescent lights are miles above me. The space is as wide-open as the world or a hungry mouth.

The wolf responds a moment after my body, and it is within this delay that I metamorphose. I become big and exaggerated. I heave my shoulders forward, one, then the other, and I drag my claws against the ground because I know how to slink. Teeth as big as thimbles peek out from my gums. I keep my head low behind the cheerleaders and pitch my body forward when the trumpets blare.

No one speaks to me when I am the wolf, and I do not speak to them: I am all beast or all girl. I see the world in flashes as though through the slats of a wicker basket and respond by instinct to the familiar pattern of the band—advance, retreat, advance, retreat, advance-advance-advance-*attack!*

I rush the opposing team: this is something of a transgression. Rival mascots may come to soft blows in the passion of a time-out, but the athletes, jerseys hanging from their bodies like jewels, are a sacred species. It happens that my arm brushes against the soft flesh of Number 3. He jumps at the touch of my knotted hair. The referee blows his silver whistle. The monochrome crowd rises to my defense like a flood.

The cheerleaders are circling around me, now, red skirts lashing against hairless legs. They are flowers. They are sundrops. They are cursive letters. They spend more time in the air than on the ground, flying in elegant arcs like fish from a pot of boiling water—and I am their dark contrast. Our beauty/ferocity is exquisite symbiosis, and as I break free from their tenuous cage of bodies, I make them shimmer and flex.

Air comes to me in hot, desirous gasps as we approach the climax of our Thursday-night rite. The observers in the stands add fever to fire, pushing forward onto the gymnasium floor. I perch on my back legs and lift my nose to the sky: the music cuts to nothing, and the crowd joins in my spectacular howl.

When our routine is finished and the game is won, I change with the cheerleaders in the women's locker room. Off come my hairy hands, claws mere facsimile of ferocity; off comes my head with the yellow eyes stitched by careful needle. I feel the zipper pinch against my belly like the suggestion of a knife, and the wolf falls away.

I emerge clothed in skin-tight black garments, my frame that of a gymnast or a child. The other girls have to blink their eyes to adjust. They rearrange their bodies and remember that I am fourteen and sweet-tempered as a sugar-spun lamb.

"Oh, hello," they say. "There you are."

DAUGHTERS

JENNIFER L. HARRISON   SEATTLE, WASHINGTON, US

did we transcend
oil-stained filling stations
fried spam, the promise of Jesus
the pressure of unwanted hands
on our untouched skin

night stretching
her heavy monochrome blanket
across swamp and hayfields
dragging down the orange melt
of Georgia's pine-pierced sky

did we stomp the red earth
under our bare, stained feet

howl

into the ever

                silence

to wake our Mother
to be sure we were ourselves

like the splintered light

coming through?

*

where I come from you have
a daughter

dandelions tangled
in suspenders

you have a daughter
up on her toes

reaching
for the sun

RISING

TAMRA PALMER   MARRICKVILLE, NSW, AUS

By the time Marian glanced up from her phone, they were already a long way up.

It had been a rushing kind of morning. After peeling the teenager off the couch and pushing him out the door, she'd had no time to clean up the place, let alone any time for herself before she had to get to the shopping centre.

God knows what I look like, she thought, rolling her eyes. *If only they sold better fruit at the supermarket, I wouldn't even have to go up to Wild+Fresh to get those fucking avocados.*

As she stepped on the escalator, she pulled out her phone. As usual, there were no calls or texts from Gary. A *pfhht* sound escaped her lips. Marriage had emptied out all of his spontaneity. It was as if, like a woman's eggs, he'd been born with only a certain amount of light-hearted communication and he'd used it all up. If she got a message from him now, she'd think someone had died rather than it possibly being a funny video or a *how r u?*

Marian scrolled through the usual sumptuous food photos from Georgina. *How* she had time to make all those extravagant meals, style them, photograph, and presumably eat them, she'd never know. She couldn't imagine Georgina ever having a toasted cheese sandwich. It would be against her culinary religion! Someone would have to forcibly restrain her, prise open her reluctant mouth and force it down. Even Georgina's 'simple' meals were complicated with rare ingredients no one had ever heard of.

'Fennel pollen. Berbere. Nigella seed,' Marian murmured softly to herself like an incantation.

The exotic words felt wrong to say out loud, as if she was pretending to be someone she wasn't. A mark on her blouse caught her eye: a small oil stain amongst the paisley flowers. Peanut butter from this morning. She sighed deeply and scrolled on.

Janice and Susie had both been on recent trips, and there were endless lovely holiday snaps showing smiling faces and heavily saturated sunsets. She hadn't known Susie could jetski, but there you go.

Marian wiped her hand down the side of her jeans. She was starting to get that grubby feeling; an anger mixed with desire that made her feel like she'd watched pornography or something. She felt a kind of digital grime building on her fingers as she scrolled and pressed down over and over.

Enough. She looked up and saw that the escalator was still going up. By now, they should have arrived at the second level, but instead, they were rising above the centre. Her small, brown eyes widened. She gripped the rubber handrail tighter as it chugged along beside her, humming with industry.

What's going on? She blinked. *I must be dreaming.*

She pinched herself hard on the forearm, but all that did was confirm it bloody well *hurt*. Her neck cracked as she twisted to look down: her shopping was still there at her feet, and far below was another woman on the same escalator. She whipped back round, panting in disbelief. Above her, the steel combed stairs seemed to rise indefinitely; a silver road into the sky.

Maybe I'm having a brain aneurysm?! she thought, her hand cradling her forehead. *My perspective's all off.*

She sat down on the cool, metal step and looked at her phone. Her finger hovered over the zero. It would be embarrassing if they arrived and found her standing on the second level with her shopping, all fine and simply *hormonal*. Colourful heat rose to her cheeks as if on cue. She looked around again, but they were still rising, even further up now so that she could see the whole of the outside car park.

The phone rang and rang, but no one from emergency services answered.

'WHAT'S HAPPENING?!' she yelled, but the words seemed to evaporate as soon as they left her mouth.

Meanwhile, the impossible escalator continued climbing into the sky—an Escher painting like the one she'd had on her teenage bedroom wall—the stairs that led up and down at the same time. *That's it!* She grabbed her shopping bags and started to climb down the stairs. In a minute, she'd reach that other woman and they'd work out what to do together.

'Hello!' she called down to her. 'Hello there!!'

But no matter how many stairs she descended, the distance between them stayed the same. She went faster, trying to outrun the climbing escalator, but she wasn't dressed for speed. For some reason, that morning she'd chosen her red, strappy sandals with the small heel.

'Stupid! Bloody! Shoes!'

Eventually she stopped; puffing, her armpits moist, the shopping bags cutting into her hands like punishment. Her heart pounded inside its cage. She watched as the other woman far below tried to do the same thing: turning and climbing down the steps, but just like her, she seemed to be walking on the spot, making no progress, going nowhere.

A tiny bird fluttered in Marian's stomach. It was getting colder the higher they rose, and the hair on her forearms bristled. She put down the heavy bags and rubbed her skin, then gripped her soft upper arms in a firm embrace. The tiny bird inside her beat its wings, trying to get out. Marian leant over the edge and screamed,

'*HELP! HELP! HEEELLLLP!*'

But she could see they were too far gone. Far below, people were just tiny dots. Cars were simply larger dots moving around, and everything looked like the cross-stitch her mother had forced her to do when she was young, with different-coloured sections chosen for here and there. Yellow for fields of grain. Blue for the sea.

This time she took off her shoes, left the bags behind, and ran as fast as she could down the stairs. It didn't change anything. She looked down at the shopping still at her feet.

When she threw the first apple, she thought she would see it fall all the way down, but she would never know its final resting place or hear the satisfying splatter. She threw another and another.

'Surely *someone* will look up and wonder why it's raining *fucking fruit*?!'

Tears pricked her eyes, and she slumped again on the metal step. When she waved to the woman below, in something like solidarity, she realised she was making a strange, soft *errrh eeerrrh* sound to go with her actions, like the muted way she yelled at people in traffic from inside her car. *Stupid woman*, she thought, *no wonder people can't hear me.*

The other woman waved back, but she was too far away to distinguish any features. Marian couldn't tell what she was feeling, but her wave seemed half-hearted and a little broken somehow.

The shopping bag was open beside her, and she saw the last of the rosy-pink apples she'd bought on special. They were almost in season. Soon, she realised, she'd be unpacking her woollen jumpers and corduroy pants and have that usual feeling of excitement, quickly followed by disappointment. Her clothes would appear at first like wonderful old friends, then appraised anew, like annoying relatives.

The first bite was unexpectedly juicy, and some of it ran out the corners of her mouth and dribbled down her chin, following the contours of her neck all the way to her cleavage. She closed her eyes and grinded the sweet flesh between her teeth until it disappeared. When she opened them again, she could see the ocean ahead: a huge blue expanse fringed with white. It looked impossibly big and more impressive somehow than all the buildings and highways below. Was that the tang of salt in the air? She breathed deeply, filling her lungs, and her mind went to Tahiti. Her secret desire. The name had always sounded so exotic, and if only Gary had been more imaginative, they could have spent time together in a kind of paradise. It was too late now. Her best years were behind her, ones where she could have worn a sarong and swum naked in the night. She stood, still taking in the salty air, and gazed across to the other side. In the distance, beyond the grid-like suburbs and long, straight highways, patchwork-coloured fields gave way to rolling hills and gullies thick with green forest.

When was the last time she'd flown in an aeroplane? It must have been that trip to the Gold Coast when Louie snapped his front tooth trying to pull off a bottle top. Years. A decade. She turned back to the sea and watched the unsettled horizon.

The loud screech startled her, and she lurched, her foot slipping off the edge of the step. She clawed at the handrail, her fingernails finally digging into the firm rubber. A wave of giddy adrenaline surged through her as she pulled herself back up, gulping air, her ankle stinging from where it had scraped the metal edge.

The seagull was poised mid-air beside her, less than an arm's length away. Its pale, glassy eye was ringed in red like a tiny planet with its own corona. Its wing feathers were spread, overlocking, catching the wind that fluttered at the soft, flayed edges.

Marian thought she'd never seen anything as cleverly beautiful. The bird's small, red legs and feet were neatly extended towards its fanned tail-feathers. It reminded her of a ballet dancer mid-leap.

'Are you a sign?' she said aloud. 'Do you have a message for me?'

It didn't seem that stupid a question up here.

The seagull continued to bob and ride the wind with minor adjustments, disinclined to answer. Then it pumped its wings once and peeled away. Marian watched it disappear. Gone.

She thought of other things disappearing. Louie's face bloomed in her mind, and she felt her heart pump and swell. But it was him as a baby, reaching up to her with starfish hands, not the surly teenager he'd become. A feeling of forgiveness flowed through her like water.

A sudden, cool wisp of vapour enveloped her, and for a moment, there was nothingness. Was this how it would be now? Everything else gone too? A tendril of panic grew up her spine. But a moment later, she popped out into clear sky, and she held her mouth in relief. She could still see the land and sea and the blue dome as before. The cloud was simply below her, something she had passed through and was now above and beyond.

A sudden urge overtook her, and she reached up behind her back and unhooked her bra. Her large breasts were eagerly out of their restraints, and when she lifted her blouse, her nipples pinched in the cold, two compasses pointing to the east. She laughed aloud, then suddenly remembered the other woman. Dropping her top, she looked down, but the woman was facing away. For the first time, she realised how similar their hair colour was, and… was that a paisley top? She blinked a few times.

Maybe I'm in the Escher painting as well? she wondered. Anything seemed possible.

The light was changing. The golden afternoon glow was giving form and depth to the clouds below her, turning them into fantastical mountainscapes and buildings all curled and strange with spires and soft steeples, wispy turrets and minarets. A kingdom of light. A queendom— she reimagined—just for her. She turned a slow full circle, taking in the enormity of the view.

They were leaving the troposphere, she knew. Not that she was some kind of geography whiz. It's just she'd once helped Louie with his homework, and some things just stick in your mind: the picture in the textbook of the Earth's atmosphere with its skin-like layers. Next would be the stratosphere and then the mesosphere, where there were hardly any light molecules. Then the wide thermosphere and finally the exosphere. Then it was just space.

The first step was the hardest, but after that, she got into a nice rhythm.

As she climbed, she found herself softly singing her favourite song about another 'Marianne', who laughed and cried about it all. And she did laugh out loud to the darkening sky, and it quickly turned to a sob, but not of devastation, more like the breaking down of some final resistance, like pricking the skin that forms over hot milk, allowing her true feelings to flow out, because she could finally see everything, and was a part of it and above it all, like a goddess.

THE SMILE

JONATHAN CHIBUIKE UKAH   LONDON, UK

In the coming days,
when you are old, grey and slow in mind,
dreams packed into bags of white dust,
your greatest loves gone, leaving you behind
to ferry their ashes across the grey sea,
visit their graves with ashes on their head,
your teeth clattering at the roof of your mouth,
your palms creased by bunches of daisies,
which you toss at their grim graves
to the chagrin of their neighbours,
take this photo of your youth I tucked in your hand.

Remember the moments of honey confidence
you wrestled from the jaws of a timeless time,
the hem of your summer gown soiled by ice cream,
when you cheekily threw caution to the stars
and treated yourself to self-indulgence;
you will think little of the loudest drone
leaving behind the dust of our fortunes,
making mocking gestures of your frivolities
when you danced in the green dress I bought for you.

When the time comes, with this photo in your hands,
remember the treasures of your lovely children,
grand and great-grandchildren, trusted friends,
affection dividing their lips like the Red Sea
at the stroke of Moses' lethal weapon.
Though time has sped and gone down the sea,
stare at this photo with confidence at the sky,
and if it fails to bring back the sunshine,
sit back and hold a long, lingering smile,
and dream that my hand is still locked in yours.

A WOMAN IN HER COAT

JAZ WARD   DARLEY, VIC, AUS

Going nowhere in particular, she grabs onto its peeling yellow rail. Her head down, she navigates her way through its sea of bodies and briefcases to find the last seat—careful not to trip over herself as the floor beneath her returns to that familiar, unsteady sway. Number 35, with its golden trim; the famed City Circle tram. A passing blur of maroon in streets that don't stop. Or is it more a shade of burgundy? She doesn't really know. She was never good with colours. Whatever is most like her late-night glass of red.

Monday to Sunday, all morning and all afternoon, the number 35 City Circle tram of red-wine colour makes its way around Melbourne's periphery. Then again. And again. Like clockwork. Like a blood vessel, taking everybody where they need to go. Oxygenating the body, the city.

On the outside, there is this bustle, a forever chaos of suits and junkies and tourists, and teenagers in their tight tops and short skirts. But on the inside, there is this momentary pause of time. It is this perpetual stillness within a city of millions, this suspension of everything that she longs for. Craves. It's almost like those scenes in those movies with the guy and his dope, where everything slows down in a world that is too fast. There, on the flaking leather benches beside etched glass windows, she can just be. Oh, how she could sit there forever. Just being.

For hours she is there, in that tram. Thinking about nothing. Thinking about everything. Thinking about how the man standing beside the platform door reminds her of somebody that she used to know. Thinking of how beautiful the city is, in its palette of autumn colour. Thinking about her husband, who won't think to cook dinner for them, for her. Thinking about the people she can see from her window, wondering where they have been and where they will go. A lady in fur and dark eyeliner smokes a cigarette, crouched by the pavement. A boy runs with his shoelaces undone, hand stretched for his father's. Thinking about how, for a moment, they are there, and then they are not. Swallowed by the metropolis.

Thinking about how she's rather invisible in this tram, in this city. In this life.

She wasn't always like this; a woman hidden within her coat. Twenty-something years ago she was just another one of those girls who thought the city was hers. Big dreams. Even bigger heels. Oh, how naive she was.

From her open window, the cold air carries an all-too-familiar echo of girlish screams. Even above the noise of the tram and the cars and the people, she can hear them. Their squeals, their laughter.

And then she sees them. It was her. Who she used to be. Young girls in a big city, no care in the world. She smiles, watching them dance through crowds of ordinary people, weightless. Lost in time, or more so, free of its burden. Young and wild. And for a moment, she is that girl again.

But then the tram turns. Inevitably. The verve of Flinders Street behind her. Now where the sun cannot quite reach, what would be scenes of Spring Street are reflections in the carriage windows. She stares back at herself. Under its flickering luminaire, she can see the greys she tries to hide. The lines around her mouth. And above her brows. The circles under her eyes, poorly painted by drugstore concealer.

Just a woman hidden within her coat. An old woman. A sad woman. Is this really what she looks like to the world? Do they see me? She turns away, and the screams of the girls grow faint. Almost indistinct amongst the noise of everything. Until they are eventually lost in the loud chorus of the city.

It's almost bittersweet, watching the day begin to end. The old Victorian buildings turn golden, bricks glistening. The edges of window panes crystalise in the changing air. Scarves are wrapped tightly around cold necks. Neon-lettered signs change from open to closed. And everything seems tired; the people, the trees, the clouds. Feet numb, it's time for her to go home.

She waits for Spencer Street. The walk to Southern Cross Station is not far. Head down, she makes her way to its platform door. But now, she understands the rhythm of the carriage's sway. Her legs move with the shudders and the shakes of its wheels meeting cobblestone. Then the door opens; migrations of people coming and going. Old and young. Slow and fast. Polite and impolite. Anyone and everyone. In the moment of chaos, she grabs onto the peeling yellow rail and steps off. Returned to an unmoving ground. Her hand speckled with its rusting paint.

And the tram leaves, a blur of maroon once more in streets that don't stop. And it will return tomorrow, with or without her, like clockwork. And again, and again. And the autumn leaves will turn brown and litter the streets, kissing grey pavements. And those girls dancing in crowds of ordinary people will be girls no more. And they will grow old and hide themselves in their coats.

And they will understand, inevitably, why she would sit on the number 35 tram. Just being.

HOSPITALS & HEALTH

UNDER THE INDIFFERENT RAIN

CATALINA STERIU BUCHAREST, ROMANIA

It was our second year of medicine, and we were attending the first dissection on a human body, whispers the man seated on the edge of the hospital bed. He has rounded shoulders, and he is watching the floor. The bags under his eyes are like two leeches that have stepped out from the bushes of his grey beard. He passes his hand through his tangled hair.

It's been almost thirty years, but it seems like yesterday. Maybe because, lately, I recall more and more my beginnings. Just imagine, Robert, he tells the young doctor beside him.

The big lecture theatre was full of young energy. Blonde buns, braided tails, inexperienced young men whose hands had not yet known the flesh, other than from the anatomy manuals. A big momentum of vitality. Down in front of us was our professor, a short and hunchbacked man, who was babbling on about medicine. He was making large gestures with his hands in surgical gloves, in front of a table covered with a white bedsheet. The agitation in the benches was interrupted and replaced by a general 'Wow' when the professor vigorously pulled the corner of the bedsheet, unveiling the yellowish corpse of a man in his forties. Rather old, I had said to myself at that moment.

Dear Robert, when you are in your twenties, you believe that people in their forties have seen everything, and they can already retire quietly on curly clouds in order to play harp sonatas.

In the lecture theatre, an invisible sponge erased smiles instantly. Silence was taking control like a king installed on his throne in front of his subjects. It looked a lot like *The Anatomy Lesson of Dr Nicolaes Tulp* by Rembrandt. The lips of everyone were frozen because of this first frontal encounter with death, the mysterious enemy they would have to fight every day from that moment. They would have to prevent, at all costs, this gardener from cutting the fresh or the faded roses from the big terrestrial park. The professor's voice echoed again in the stunned lecture theatre. He needed a volunteer to take the scalpel. A rustle crossed over the benches. I touched my cheeks. They seemed to be two hot buns. I only looked up when I heard the heels. It was her, Robert. With a majestic attitude, she was heading towards the professor, without any hesitation, while she was fixing her blonde hair. She approached the professor, and this was the moment when I saw her face for the first time. A poppy in a field of wheat. The brown eyes on her oval doll face were curiously examining the body. I was sure that if she were to kiss the unfortunate man lying on the table, he would return to life. Suddenly the doors of my heart were too noisy, and I didn't understand why. The girl took the scalpel. 'Let's start with the clavicle,' urged the professor. Her small, white hands already at work. Those beautiful and powerful hands, which would remove so many lives from the claws of our common enemy, will now pass their silky shell to someone else, explains the doctor to Robert. He takes the hand of the woman in bed connected to the ventilator. He grasps her long and cold fingers and kisses them, to transfer to her a little bit of his warmth.

With tears in his eyes, the young Robert leaves the room.

Left alone, the man takes off his white medical clogs and lies near the woman's inert body. He caresses her long hair, her big forehead, the eyelids that are hiding for good the black diamonds which sparked each time a life had been saved. He lets the memories flow at the same time, with his warm tears on the pillow. In his dream, he relives their wedding in Nice, on the French Riviera, and he sees again his wife having the same assurance in her gestures that exhaled confidence, dressed in a white butterfly-like dress. And then he remembers the hundreds of surgical interventions, shoulder to shoulder, sharing the sweet joy but also some defeats in front of the black cape, including that of their unborn daughter. The suffering like a bitter cough syrup and then the pain generated by the incapacity to have other children coexisted in the soul of his wife, together with hope and faith that one day she would succeed in giving birth. Little by little, as years went by, the curiosity of discovering the world as they travelled together replaced the pain. They had started to climb Everest with five friends, and it was she who had finished it first while he had been the last one to accomplish it. In their travels on the Mediterranean Sea, she was always the first one to dive into the water and swim. He also recalled their trip to Lapland, where he was trembling because it was minus 26 degrees Celsius under the aurora borealis, which resembled a green and purple tornado, while she jumped like a white hare in the piles of snow. A long row of adventures on unknown and distant lands, brutally interrupted in their very town. The motorcycle, the city lights reflecting on the wet pavement like candles in the darkness of a church, the crouched body under the indifferent rain.

I alone will take care of you, my darling. I wouldn't stand the hands of other doctors, our colleagues, to touch your smooth skin, your eyes, your liver, your kidneys, even your bones or your heart, big enough for all the patients in the world. You used to say that you didn't succeed in giving birth. Now, the time has come. And you will give birth not to one person, but to seven other people, who will survive thanks to you. Tomorrow I will take the scalpel. And I will do it like you did thirty years ago: confident and sure of myself, in the name of life.

REVIVING ANGELO

EVI RUHLE   MELBOURNE, VIC, AUS

A woman is wailing, but the man at the counter assures me I'm in the right place. His voice is hushed. He isn't even wearing a medical uniform.

'Is this your first time?' While he fumbles with the paperwork, I look around so as not to pressure him.

Patients look up from their beds as if accusing me of disturbing them, but they're probably just bored. Or unwell. There must be twenty stations, but I can't see everyone through the partitions. A nurse walks me to what will be my camp for the next few hours and draws the curtains around me. A splash of turquoise against the grey-and-white surfaces that inhibit bacterial growth. While I wait for her to return, I close my eyes to unsee the neon lights. Breathing is what you're meant to do. I imagine myself floating in the ocean on my back, letting the waves take control.

Behind the curtain to my left, a man apologises to a nurse mopping up the floor.

'I couldn't help it. It comes on real quick.' The words tumble out of his mouth over and over. Then he laughs. In embarrassment, I think.

'It's okay. It's the catheter. It makes your bladder lazy.' The nurse calms him. 'It takes a while to get going. A bit like me in the morning before my second coffee.' She uses the panacea of humour.

It's working on me, and I reopen my eyes. I push myself back up on the slippery grey vinyl of my chair. A woman in her own chair across the way has given in to an almost horizontal position, her eyes on the needle in her arm, perhaps watching the infusion trickle through the tube into her vein, into her body. I get more upright still and wrap the cardigan tighter around myself. You wouldn't think it's 40 degrees outside.

Nurses crisscross the ward. An army of blue. In their tending to the patients, they are efficient but not rushing. Masked-up, they appear homogeneous, and I have to guess their lives by their mannerisms and voices. Some of them smile with their eyes. I squint back to encourage their encouragement.

After the diagnosis, I was scared and angry. At least now I know why my leg misbehaves sometimes. Why stars flash before my eyes. Best to keep busy. I can't log onto the wi-fi, but I don't want to bother the nurses. I manage to load old copies of *The Economist*. A chance to step back in time. But I soon tire of yesterday's news. I want to know what happens tomorrow. How I'll do in the future.

'I'll give you the premeds and measure your blood pressure. It's very straight forward,' the nurse says with an Irish accent. While she fits me with the needle and adjusts my drip, we chat about Ireland and the pros and cons of living fifteen thousand kilometres away from family. When I'm hooked up, I scroll through the downloaded audio books on my phone. My childhood's tongue lulls me into a daze. Until a machine beeps on my right and another chimes in from my left, like two robot birds communicating. Some patients are freed from their tubes and are gathering their things.

The buzz at the counter has subsided. Staff must be lunching, and there has been a shift change. A skinny man in plain clothes waters two puny pot plants on the counter. He has an un-Australian knack at nursing them, helping them survive. Something organic against the sterility.

I'll be able to walk among trees for a long time to come, my new nurse assures me as she doubles my dose. The plastic bladder dangling from the trolley's pole to my left looks limp. I have sucked some of the life from it. That life is now inside me.

The Irish nurse has returned with a cappuccino from downstairs. 'Because it's your first time,' she whispers and draws the curtain around me. Probably to hide the coffee. The curtain continues to swing after she's gone. The other patients have to make do with the instant coffee from the kitchenette. She's not supposed to have favourites, but I lap up the simple kindness. My mum rings me every second day. It's normal I'm told. We try and bridge the distance with video calls. 'You should come home,' she tries. 'So we can look after you.' I don't tell her about the older people here, in their linty washed-out trackies. I know she's thinking that'll be my plight. I don't want it to rub off on me.

A woman picks her way past my bed with her walking stick. I try and garner a sense of mobility from the plane passing above. I will visit home eventually and explain everything to Mum. All she has is an encyclopedia that's twenty years old, and it feeds her outdated information about the disease. No wonder she's worried. If only she knew how to use a computer. My friend from school has begun to communicate with me through Messenger. The photos of parties and holidays she posts on social media look exotic. I look forward to knocking back a few cocktails with her when I get over there. Our teenage shenanigans seem distant. I wish myself back into her Beetle, parked on the gravel next to the *route nationale*, doubling as a night's shelter on our way to Spain. The unfelt discomfort of tossing and turning side-by-side on our folded-down car seats while trucks hurtled past outside. Three countries in twenty-four hours in that little car.

The afternoon seems less frantic and the unknown settles into a routine. The nurse tells me I'll be able to make my own way home, and I'm glad I don't have to trouble my partner. Many patients are gone, their beds and infusion trolleys now spick and span. With some of the curtains folded back, I get a better view of the row of windows that looks out onto the main road. The first cars kick off the rush hour. As they idle at the red light, heat glimmers around them in the sun. I'm grateful I live near the beach.

Another hour or two. People have told me writing can be cathartic. I've never fully made friends with that word. Who wants to hear about hospitals? I'd prefer to write about driving through Europe, eating *éclairs au chocolat* and scoring dope in San Sebastián. But when I look around, I realise right now this is my reality. It's not forever. I get out my laptop, and I'm willing to give it a go. I pick through my brain for any clues on how to start. Lucia Berlin comes to mind. I have always found it hard to think of her as American with a surname like that. One of her stories is set in a laundromat. Her writing fills that mundane place with life and compassion, gives it a role for those relying on it. For laundering or just some company. Perhaps I can manage that. Give my diagnosis some sort of meaning to stop it from niggling me. As I begin to tap what I see around me into the keyboard, I develop a distance to my emotions. I've even managed to adjust the footrest so that I'm no longer sliding down on my chair.

I've tried before to write things down but have lacked the energy. Now the words flow from my mind through my fingers onto the keyboard with a focus that has left me many years ago or that I might have never had in the first place. I can't remember.

The bed of the man who had lost control of his bladder is now occupied by a lanky guy dressed in black. His matching hair hangs down to his shoulders in greasy streaks. When I say *hi*, I fool myself that I'm his age. He asks what I'm tapping away at. I tell him I'm updating my CV. He chuckles at my eagerness and says that the focus comes from the premeds, the steroids.

'I get my best remixes done in here. Just waiting for the nurse to come and administer my dose.'

Our laptops give us something in common. 'Are you a musician?' I ask. 'Yeah.' He nods. 'And a DJ.' He adjusts the noise-cancelling headphones over his ears.

I wonder to myself whether I could get a script for steroids.

My new nurse tells me she's from Ghana. As she clips a curl behind the straps of her mask, she explains my blood pressure won't read and asks me to uncross my feet. I apologise, to which she giggles. When she doubles my dose for the last time, I almost panic. My writing becomes a race against the infusion bag draining the last of its elixir into me. I need to make the most of this extraordinary focus, this opportunity to write down what I see and feel while I'm in the midst of it. I hammer the keyboard with my fingers for a good fifteen minutes until the machine next to me beeps. The muso doesn't take his eyes off the virtual audio mixer on his screen. His body is pulsing back and forth. When the nurse tells me I need to stay an extra hour for observation, I'm relieved and continue refining what now could pass as a story.

'There, you're done,' the nurse says as she finally extracts the needle from my arm.

I'm done indeed, I think to myself and close my laptop, happy with what I've written. As I pack up, I try not to wake the guy in black, but when I heave my bundle onto my back, he pops up his head.

'Ready to go home?'

I've grown tired of small talk but reply. 'Yes, how about you? Do you have much longer?'

'Staying overnight for observation.'

Before I can say I'm sorry, he asks, 'What were you really writing?' His eyes are puffy.

From the headphones abandoned on the side table, tinny drumbeats fade in and out. Lying won't do, and I come clean about the story.

'What's it about?' he asks.

'Just about this ward. For something to do.'

'Am I in it?'

I hesitate.

'Might be my only chance to ever leave this place.'

I'm not sure whether he's using humour. I don't want to say the wrong thing.

'I can live on in your story.' He adjusts his mask and briefly reveals his face, which locks babyish. 'If you published it.'

'It's not that sort of a story,' I say, way too serious.

A nurse is unlocking the wheels of his bed.

'Let's get you to the other ward.'

When she hands him over to a man in a grey uniform, she speaks matter-of-factly. 'Good luck.' The muso waves at me as he's being wheeled away. He's no longer wearing his street clothes but is swaddled in one of the white hospital gowns.

On the tram, I regret never having asked his name. The world isn't flying past as usual but crawling in the heat. Across from me, a school kid, too young to be out alone, has a mobile phone pressed to his ear, assuring the invisible interlocutor he'll be home in ten minutes. As he spins his excuse, his eyes sparkle with confidence. Superhero figurines dangle from his school bag, among them, a nametag signed Angelo.

Back home, I'm thinking about the muso confined to his hospital bed. And him asking me whether he featured in my story. I decide to give him a go:

A woman is wailing, but the man at the counter assures Angelo he's in the right place. Angelo smiles.

THE CLOCK READS

NIAMH KELLEHER   WAHROONGAH, NSW, AUS

9:48pm the clock reads before it flies past. I lie resolutely on my back, staring blankly at the ceiling as uniform-clad figures rush past me, gripping the wheeled bed and pulling me along as if I was a broken ragdoll. The cold draught of the hallway bites my skin, mirroring the icy feeling settled in my stomach as the shriek of sirens still rings in my ears hauntingly. The voices of reassuring doctors rush through my head, but angst worms its way into my thoughts, causing their soothing faces to swim in front of my eyes mockingly. The jostling that comes with every turn of the corridors and the hushed whispers that follow me like a cloud of agitated bees until I finally halt.

A gallery of whitewashed walls and faded blue doors greets me. The reek of disinfectant clouds the senses as my eyes drowsily graze over the sterile environment. The faint scratching of a nurse's pen as it flies across a page I cannot see as a chorus of heart monitors echo throughout the ward, their beeps like a choir of the dead singing eerily. I scan the room for its occupants; adolescents dripping in a tangle of cords, IV drips and tubes hang limply around the room. Their eyes weary and yet… glowing with hope and peace as they sit silently on their beds, reading or gazing out the window.

A mousy-haired girl sits bundled in hospital blankets, nose almost entirely submerged in her book, no doubt immersed in a land of wonder. A green-eyed young boy in a wheelchair, earphones plugged in, quietly swaying to a song only he can hear. My brow furrows slightly, in subtle awe. I wonder how, in the midst of this dank, morose hospital, lie young souls still thriving in contentment. Again, I spot a seemingly mid-teenage girl with closely shaven hair, sketching in a leather-bound journal, a smile tugging at her lips. A child with hair as vivid as flames, leaning against the window and gazing towards the star-strewn sky in wonder. Roaming the room, my eyes catch a pair of warm brown eyes. A smile curves his lips as he nods as if to say, *'you'll be ok.'* I manage a small smile in return before sinking into my bed, breathing a sigh of acceptance. I glance up. 9:49pm the clock reads.

PUNCTURE

CAITLIN MAHONY   BACCHUS MARSH, VIC, AUS

Tom saw her from across the road. She coasted on her bike, delicate long limbs, skin golden and smooth. Kicking a leg over, she stood on one pedal, seemingly pulled by a magnetic force towards the bike rack. Kids in rashies, dogs on leads, sandals, sunscreen, all became a kaleidoscope of shapes, colours, and smells he didn't notice. A supermarket button-up shirt hugged her torso, flattered her breasts. She disappeared through the automatic door. He breathed in the salty air.

Slumped on the couch, Tom was already feeling edgy. The cricket on TV was a hypnotising dance of bowling, batting, bowling, batting. Too many long, empty days. Velvet couch fabric against his arms and legs itched.

'Hey, Tom,' said his grandma from the kitchen.

'Ya.'

'Can I make you a sandwich, love?'

'Oh, yeah. I mean, yes, please.'

The heat was building. He felt himself starting to sweat. He got up, lumbered to the pedestal fan and switched it to three, then fell back on the couch.

Grandma entered, accompanied by her rose perfume, treading well-worn carpet, gripping Tom's plate. Her hands wore manicured nails.

'Now that's the last of the ham. If you want any tomorrow, you'll need to pop down to the shops.'

Tom bit into the white bread. Ham, cheese, and butter on both sides, just the way he liked it. His mother always bought the grainy bread—that was before she went to hospital. Before Tom landed here, in limbo between childhood and adulthood, too old to need taking care of, too young to be out on his own. A fledgling. He was glad Grandma had insisted he stay with her, but he was stuck at the end of the world with no friends, no money, no job, and he felt pretty useless.

'Now, I found this empty card in the drawer. You should write to your mother.'

He took the card and opened it to reveal a blank inside. He felt his heart sink as he thought of writing in it. Writing to her. Putting it on paper and making it all real.

'Maybe later,' he said and took another bite.

As a kid, Tom remembered summer trips to Grandma and Grandpa's house. He would help his mum load the boot of their station wagon, a jigsaw of bags, board games, and beach stuff. Pillows on top. Tom would sit in the back seat with their Jack Russell, Pippa. When he was a bit older and when Pippa was a lot older, he would sit in the front, Pippa still in the back seat. Until the summer when she wasn't there anymore.

Arriving at Grandma and Grandpa's, he was welcomed by the smell of mothballs. Itchy hugs up against Grandpa's woollen vest and a soft hug wrapped in Grandma's arms. Days filled with salt and sun; evenings sitting at the dinner table with sunburn, playing board games. Tom would usually lose, but he would draw little love hearts on the scorecard to make his mother smile.

Tom and Grandma sat at the dinner table. Bangers, mash and peas. They ate silently. The ghost of Grandpa at the head of the table. The weight of his mother's hospital stay filled the room.

'Have you heard anything from Mum's doctors today?' asked Tom.

'No, nothing, but I'm sure she'd appreciate a card.' She stabbed a piece of sausage and lifted it to her mouth.

Tom stared into space, thinking about how he had nothing to fill that blankness.

Grandma finished chewing. 'Tom?'

'Yeah, yeah, I'll think about it.'

'She'd be lonely in there. I think it would brighten her day.'

Tom thought about seeing her in there, how she was barely awake the whole time. Would she even read it? Would she even notice? What would he say anyway? He scoffed down the rest of his meal. He shouldn't be here; he should be in Melbourne with her. It felt hard to breathe.

He'd done the trip by public transport once in the time he'd been staying at Grandma's. During the bus ride, he felt more and more light-headed until he arrived at Geelong Station. Then spent a long wait recalibrating his head and staring at the glowing contents of the vending machine. Why would anyone buy one of those cardboard biscuits with so many better options available?

On the train, his light-headedness came back. After each station, they'd pick up speed and his guts would start to churn. Keep breathing.

A young guy sat in his berth and started eating a hamburger. The smell of meat and grease made his guts turn even worse. When they reached Spencer Street Station, Tom sucked in the grey-tasting air and felt some relief. On the tram to the hospital on unsteady legs, he tried not to lunge at every abrupt stop. Queasy.

The hospital was bright, smelling of antiseptic and old age. Behind the reception desk stood a young nurse with yellow-blonde hair that flicked out at the bottom.

'I'm here to see Josie Hickney,' he said.

'Room 512, up the elevator to Level 5.' She pointed with a pen.

At his mother's door, he wondered if he should have bought flowers from the downstairs shop, or a shiny helium balloon with *Get Well Soon* printed in rainbow text. He opened the door. His mother lay there, with an audience of machines displaying lights and numbers. She looked so small.

The whole way back, he gnawed on his fingernails and tried not to vomit.

It was early evening. Another day of nothing coming to a close, passing time watching a ship enter The Heads. Tom sat on the promenade wall, feet dangling over lapping waves, toes gripping thongs. His hands ran over the rough concrete. Seaweed scent. A huge container ship, steady and enormous, dwarfing everything. Hot rays of sun seared. Tom squinted behind his sunglasses and felt the sting of sun on his already sunburnt forearms.

He passed through the automatic doors, into the air conditioning. Would the girl on the bike be working tonight? The supermarket was pretty empty for the pre-dinner rush. All those holiday-makers must be getting Friday-night takeaway—wouldn't that be nice. He felt sad as he thought about getting Chinese on Friday nights with his mum. Honey-soy chicken, sweet and sour pork, fried rice and a bag of prawn crackers. Pops of bacon in the fried rice were like little nuggets of salty gold, hidden amongst the rice and peas. There were always too many prawn crackers. Mum would only eat a few, and he would be left on the couch after dinner, crunching and covered in pink crumbs. Can't let them go to waste; they'll go soggy.

He gripped his deli ham and joined the one queue for the two checkouts. She was there, behind one of the counters. Flicking ponytail, beaded bracelet. Tom felt a hollow inside his chest as he half-wished to be served by her, half-wished he'd get the regular guy. He felt suddenly conscious about how he was standing. Weight on one foot. Too effeminate? Firm feet, crossed arms, package of meat in the crook of an elbow seemed strange. He hoped he remembered deodorant this morning.

'Next,' she said. She was standing in front of him. 'Had a good day today?' She smiled sweetly, slightly tilting her head.

'Haven't done much, just watched one of those big ships coming through The Heads.'

Why *big ships*? Why not *container ships*? Why ships at all? He felt sweat beading on his forehead.

She laughed. 'That's cool.'

On the street, he knew he should head back to Grandma's, but he needed some more time. *That's cool.* He let the echo of her laugh ripple through him. Without thinking, he crossed the road and stared into the bay, soaking in the view, plastic bag by his side, limp and mostly empty. The ship had made progress, well on its way to port in Melbourne, the last moments of its long journey. He watched for a long time, trying to imagine what it would be like to spend weeks or months at sea. Families of seagulls and humans lounged in the evening heat.

The shadows grew longer, and he decided to head back the long way. Familiar roads, unfamiliar kids on bikes and families walking dogs. A bell tinged behind him. He turned to see her. Straight back, hair catching the evening light. She passed. Then it happened.

Over a speed hump, her bag bumped out of the pannier rack and flipped as it fell to the road. Before he could think, he was running for the bag.

'Hey! Hey! You, there! On the bike!' he said.

Her brakes squeaked as she came to a stop, turning, a flash of confusion across her face. He picked up the bag, and her confusion shattered into a grin. She did a U-turn swiftly, smoothly. Mounted on her bike she was beside him.

'You know, I'd lose my head if it wasn't screwed on,' she said.

He stared up at her and handed her bag back.

'Oh, I know you,' she said. 'Just served you, right? Ham? Oh wait, did I just break server–customer confidentiality?'

'Oh.' He laughed. 'No, it's fine.'

'You a local or what? Don't strike me as a holiday-maker.'

'Yeah, well, kinda. I suppose you could call me a temporary resident.'

'Temporary resident. I like that. I'm gonna steal that. I'm just staying here for now until I sort something else out.'

'Same.' He scratched his head.

'Anyway, thanks for the bag. See ya around. I'm Chelsea.'

'No worries.'

She started riding away.

'And I'm Tom,' he shouted.

'Catch ya round, Tom.' She waved without turning around.

He felt his hands clench and noticed he was smiling. Chelsea.

The next time he saw her, the streetlights had already come on; she was kneeling next to her bike on the corner near the shops. He didn't want to seem like a creep, but maybe she needed some help.

'Hey, Chelsea!' he said.

She turned quickly and rose to her feet, gripping her hands in fists.

'Sorry, I didn't mean to scare you. It's Tom. From your bag, from ham.'

'Oh, hi, Tom.' She released her fists and put her hands on her hips. 'I've got a flat.'

'Oh, damn. Can I help?'

'Nah, I've got a puncture repair kit at home. Just gonna walk.' She wiped her hands on her pants.

'I'll walk you,' Tom said before thinking, then blushed. Hopefully she didn't notice.

'It's okay. It's not far. I'll be fine.'

'I don't mind.'

'Alright then.'

They walked side-by-side along the street. House windows revealed snapshots of strangers' evenings. Behind a tall wooden fence, a yard hummed with chatter and glasses clinking. No cars passed by.

'So, why are you really here anyway?' she asked.

'You mean, stalking the streets of Point Lonsdale at night? I'm staying with my grandma. I just like to get out of the house sometimes. There's only so much televised tennis I can handle.'

'Fair enough, but I mean, like, why are you here in the first place?'

'Right.' He took a breath. 'My mum's sick. In the hospital in Melbourne. I didn't really want to be stuck in the house on my own, so I came down here.'

Crickets chirped in the grass beside the road. As they walked, the nearest crickets became silent, like a quiet bubble surrounding the two-people-one-bike.

'Stop,' she whispered and pointed into the tree. 'A ringtail possum.

Oh, wait, there's two!'

Tom squinted. Two small eyes stared back. 'Oh cool, they're cute.'

'I'm sorry to hear about your mum,' she said.

'Thanks.'

At Chelsea's house, she stood beside the front gate.

'Do you wanna learn how to fix a puncture?'

Tom hesitated, feeling the pull of his grandma's house. Grandma would be sitting in front of the television working on a crochet project and somehow following the tennis match.

'Sure,' he said.

They walked down the side of the house. It was pitch black, and Tom was sure he was going to trip on something, but Chelsea and her bike were leading the way, so he trusted her. One foot after another, one hand grazing the brick, the other running across the ups and downs of a wooden fence. She led him into the backyard and to the door of a small shed. She started jiggling the latch. Rusted metal groaned with resistance, then the door flung open, releasing the smell of old petrol. Click of a light switch, and the inside was showered in orange. Chelsea strode in with her bike and flipped it upside down. She moved confidently, removing the tyre and inner tube. She sat on the dusty concrete floor. Redbacks watched from the ceiling as Tom sat next to her, close enough to see, but careful not to touch her and ruin the moment.

She wedged a tube of glue between her teeth, and she rotated the bike's inner tube, listening for a leak.

'I can hold that for you,' Tom said, and she handed him the glue and continued listening.

'Found it,' she said and pointed the leak towards Tom. 'Listen.'

He heard a faint rush of wind and felt air against his ear. He nodded. She held out her hand, and Tom placed the glue into her palm. She pasted glue, stuck on the patch and told him they'd have to wait a few minutes for it to dry.

'Do you get to see your mum?' she asked.

'Not really. I don't have a licence and Grandma doesn't drive. Public transport is a pain.' He considered telling her about his motion sickness, but he didn't want to overshare.

'Yeah. True that.'

'I've been meaning to write to her, but I don't know what to say.'

'You should do it. Tell her you love her. It would mean a lot to her.'

'Maybe. I should probably head off now so Grandma doesn't worry.'

'Righto.'

She led him back through the gap beside the house, and they said their goodbyes. The temperature had dropped, so he crossed his arms, hugging them into his body. Marching home, he ignored the sounds drifting out of houses as he thought about his mother. How helpless he felt. Her, all alone in that big building. She had been the one supporting him, and now he didn't know how to reciprocate.

That night he dreamt he was on a container ship with his mother. There was a powerful storm, and the ship rocked violently, water everywhere. Both of them were soaked through. The ship lurched to the side. Tom used one hand to grip a pole and the other to hold his mum's hand. Another wave, another lurch, and still he gripped onto her hand. She started yelling for him to let her go. He held on tight, blinking against rain and ocean spray. The ship slammed into a wave and he lost his grip. She slid away into the dark and was gone.

He jolted awake. Daylight through orange curtains gave his room a sickly glow. The air felt stagnant. He opened the curtains and the windows to let in the warm breeze. Outside his window, an assembly of moonah trees. Gnarled limbs wearing deep wrinkles, with memories of a time before. Shaped by prevailing winds. A magpie sat on one of the branches, carolling good morning to the world.

The card stared up at him from the nightstand. The roses with a pink backdrop were very old-fashioned, but it didn't matter what it looked like. That white blankness inside begged to be filled. He got dressed and grabbed the card. It was mid-morning, so Grandma would probably be in the garden. He wanted to get this done without her hovering around. There were pens next to the phone. Sitting at the table, he started, *Dear Mum*, then took a breath and let the words flow out. Midway through the white space, a tear fell onto the card, but he didn't stop; he scribbled out his feelings.

Once the white was covered in a blue scrawl, Tom looked at the mess of words. The back door slid open, and Grandma entered, still wearing her gardening gloves.

'So you've finally written a card?' she said.

'Yes, Grandma.' Tom looked downwards.

'Postage stamps are in the cupboard. Would you like some brekkie?'

The card slipped into the mouth of the red postbox and clunked on the bottom. For a moment, Tom wished to get it back. To change what he'd said, fix his spelling mistakes, scribble out the love hearts he'd drawn in the corner. But it was too late. He stood tall for what felt like the first time in months.

He needed an excuse to talk to her, but he'd come into the supermarket without a plan. He stalked the aisles looking for something cheap. *Chewing gum.* She was busy checking out a large basket of items, so Tom was forced to be Mr Nice Guy and let several customers go before him to the other checkout while he waited for her. She finally printed a receipt, and he was in front of her.

'I did it. I wrote the card,' he said, smiling.

'Good on ya. Do ya wanna go for a ride or something when I knock off?'

'Sounds good. There's an old bike at Grandma's I can use, but I think it's got a flat.'

'I reckon we can do something about that.' She winked.

Tom stood on the promenade watching a container ship leave the bay. Full of stuff, ready to go out onto the open sea, ready to face unexpected weather, to visit new ports. He ripped the plastic off the packet of gum and slipped some into his mouth. It tasted minty and fresh, and the day was full of potential.

THE THINGS WE TELL OURSELVES

ZOFIA KUYPERS   KINGSFORD, NSW, AUS

The most surprising part of living through the end of the world is discovering that it is boring.

No, I must start again. I want to be truthful here. It's not true to say that boredom is the overwhelming mood; that is just the most easily identified feeling. It's the lazy description, the word that comes to mind when you find yourself stuck at home and restricted from seeing friends, family and even strangers. But if I'm being completely honest, being truthful, if I'm to sweep away that first impression and truly describe how I'm feeling, the word I would have to use is dread. Endless, constant, gnawing dread. Oh, and another correction is required; it might not be the end of the world. It feels like the world is ending, but perhaps that is just my penchant for exaggeration.

These days, I'm allowed out of my house once a day to go for a walk. I live by myself now; my children have long since created their own homes; my husband's unexpected death was long enough ago that I can think of him with happiness, and so here I am, living in my cosy cottage in the Blue Mountains. When isolation is my choice, I love it. Solitude is my treat, fuel for my soul. But when isolation is forced upon me, it turns to loneliness and I resent it greatly. I crave companionship, but I'm also fearful enough of this virus to follow the health orders to the letter; never leaving my house without a mask, giving wide berths to any stranger I may encounter on my daily walk, even as I long to stop and chat.

I try to see how long I can last inside my house before needing to leave for my walk, how long I can last before giving myself my daily treat. My goal is to last until the afternoon, but most days, I'm pulling my front door closed behind me before nine in the morning. I remind myself of the old children's book character Mr Busy who wakes up and completes an entire day's worth of activities in thirty minutes. I wake; I eat breakfast; I tidy and then my feet begin to twitch towards the door, and I find that persuasive voice in my head rationalising my desire to head off for a walk: *you love the mist, Gerty; you might as well go for your walk in the morning while the mist is still thick.* It's true, the mist is magical. It's what drew me from Sydney up into the mountains when I found myself knocking around our empty family home with no need to be surrounded by the city hustle.

I love the smell of the mountains, the eucalyptus, the pine. I love the way you get to experience seasons up here—summer is energising; autumn is recognisable; winter is frigid. But most of all, I love the mist that so often blankets the town I live in.

Each day, I walk to the same place. It's a bench on the edge of my village, perched surprisingly at the end of a cul-de-sac looking out across the Grose Valley. I often think about the local council employee who built it. There's no standard council-approved reason to put a bench here; there's no park, no bus stop, no foot traffic in need of a resting place. The only thing here is silence and beauty and every day I'm thankful for the person who came before me and recognised the beauty of it all. I found this place decades ago as a teenager visiting my grandparents and was thrilled to find it was walking distance from my new home when I moved to the mountains a few years ago.

I reached the bench a little before nine today, and sat down reverently, looking forward to enjoying the tranquillity of this place, but moments later, a woman sat down on the other end of the seat. For a few minutes, I tried to ignore her and focus on what I had come here to do, to enjoy the beauty of this place and recharge for the next twenty-four hours at home. It was useless. A seething rage was building inside me, directed at this woman who had invaded my space, who had dared to sit so close to me. I looked across the bench and stared at this woman, hoping to convey with my eyes alone that she wasn't welcome on this bench. Peering across, I noticed she was crying. The indignant rage that had been building evaporated. Her red, watery eyes, the only part of her face visible above her mask, were staring sadly out across the misty valley. I could see her misery, and for a moment, the space between us wavered and disappeared entirely—I was her; I could feel her pain and her sadness. In fact, I have been her. Only two days ago I was sitting on this bench, in that very spot, crying about the injustice of this lockdown and this virus and then chastising my inner voice for feeling so sorry for myself when, in fact, I have everything. I have my life, my health, my family and my home. How could I be brought to tears by the prospect of spending the next few months locked inside my cosy cottage. *This is hardly the war effort!* I told myself sternly. *I'm being asked to sit on my couch for a few months—surely I can rise to the occasion.*

The sound of a small sob brought me back to the bench and my unwanted companion. The stranger reached up and wiped away a tear. I shuddered inwardly. Didn't she know not to touch her face in public?

I sighed silently at the thought of all those germs that were now marching through her tear ducts and into her respiratory system. As she returned her hand dejectedly to her lap, I noticed that we had the same wedding ring. In fact, the more I looked at this woman, the more I saw of myself. The same grey hair peeping through at the temples. The same shoulders folding forward in a fashion that so horrifies my physio—another man in this world who will never fully understand that teenage girls learn to hunch forward to hide their growing chests, and that the grown women that they grow into often can't break the habit.

My heart felt for this woman and her tears. I'm so critical of myself when I cry—*stop being so pathetic!*—but so sympathetic to others. I felt the desire to help her in some way. What could I do? Noticing my attention, she turned and caught my gaze, returning it with an unguarded curiosity that surprised me. Staring into her eyes, I felt for a strange moment as though I was looking in the mirror, but as she returned to her dejected position, the feeling dissipated.

There was a sudden gust, a breeze which prodded the mist, lifted a small pile of leaves from my feet and carried them across to the feet of the woman sitting next to me.

The movement of the leaves brought my setting into focus, and I became aware that there was someone else sitting on the bench. I hadn't noticed the woman on the bench when I collapsed into it—I couldn't see much through my tears and the mist. My tears are my constant companion in this world, relentlessly embarrassing me by leaking out of my eyeballs. Sure, they're the least objectionable bodily fluid that could escape my skin sack, but still, I'd prefer them to stay encased within my body. I needed to sit; my legs had stopped responding to my brain. Not for any remarkable or exciting reason, my jerky legs had an embarrassing cause which was nearly enough in itself to make me cry again. I had attended a Zoom gym class the day before, armed with absolute determination to make this lockdown different to the last. This time, I would become more fit and more healthy, not fatter and more pathetic. But in typical form, I had misjudged the workout, overestimated my ability, and royally overdone it. So now I couldn't even walk properly.

But right now, in this moment, my tears were from frustration and anger. The rational part of my brain was telling me that my tears were not purely due to the unpleasant interaction I had just experienced with an unknown laughing man but were the inevitable result of weeks spent living with dread and suspense. My world was changing, and change is always hard to adapt to. But change encased in fear that is thrust upon you is the hardest of all. The activities that gave my life joy had been taken away, all those small things that I took for granted; meals with friends, Pilates classes, and even shopping had all been ripped away and replaced with a mistrust of strangers, an aversion to closeness and a fear of what other people could do to you by simply breathing too closely.

I had seen this jovial man a few times at the one café in town—holding court with his posse. He appears to spend his time in the queue barking orders at the barista, laughing messily and inhabiting his space with a confidence that seems to come so easily to fat, bearded men in their fifties. I didn't want to give this man any attention; it is clear to me that attention is his fuel. But the one thing I always notice is his lack of a face mask. So today, I spoke. I asked him to put on a face mask, and his casual 'Calm down, love, it's a free country' and the sad implications of his selfishness, were too much for me today. They triggered the tears, and now I was dealing with them.

'This is a beautiful place; I love the mist,' the woman across from me spoke.

This woman could have been me. We were a similar age, similar in all regards. I think I even owned the same clothes she was wearing. I sniffled in response; I didn't yet have the energy to speak.

'It's hard, isn't it?'

'Yes,' I agreed this time, causing a stronger gush of warm salty water to run down my cheeks onto the rim of my mask.

'We're living through a once-in-one-hundred-years pandemic. I think we all need to remember that. I know I do.' The woman who was so like me spoke again. 'Are you okay?'

'I am. It's stupid. I don't even know why I'm crying. I shouldn't be.'

'There's nothing wrong with crying!'

'I just. I just… I encountered a rude man who wasn't wearing a mask, and it made me so angry and sad. It's irrational.'

'Go easy on yourself. I don't think we should judge ourselves by the same standard right now. If you need to cry, go ahead. I give you permission!'

I laughed a little at that and tried to do as this woman suggested. Surprisingly, it helped, receiving permission to cry and validation for emotions that I had, up until this point, been labelling as pathetic was freeing. A load had lifted, and my tears slowed to a trickle.

I woke the next morning in my beautiful bedroom and spent a few moments enjoying the warmth of my bed. The light seeping in through the curtains had the opalescent glow that told me it was another misty morning. I thought back to my encounter with the crying woman yesterday. Somehow it had lifted my spirits. In telling this stranger that it was okay to feel sad about her life right now, it was as if I had realised the same thing. I hadn't told myself to *Buck up and get over it* last night when I sat down to another meal alone and felt an embarrassing tear fall onto the tablecloth, instead I reassured myself with a measure of empathy I usually reserved for others.

I had more energy than I had felt for weeks as I walked my daily hilly route, which wound up and down along the top of the mountain before sloping gently down towards the edge of the valley. There's a section of my walk where the footpath becomes so steep that sloped sections of path are broken by stairs. There's something about this footpath and these stairs that when I jump off them, which a woman of my age really shouldn't, for a moment I feel like I'm flying. It's a sensation I have loved since I was a teenager. When my moods are high, I often dream of jumping down long flights of stairs in one long flying leap, feeling that weightless lurch in my stomach for a blissful moment before landing again. Most days, I trudge down these steps without even recalling the delight they once gave me, but today, I jumped. A smile spread across my face, hidden under my mask, enjoying the ridiculousness of this flight of fancy.

Approaching my bench, I wondered if I would encounter the crying woman again. I saw a figure on the bench and something inside me leapt— it might be the woman again. Perhaps I could have another illicit human interaction? But as I walked closer, the distortion of the mist lessened, and I realised it was a teenage girl, shoulders hunched forward, staring at something in her hands, a phone no doubt. I sat quietly on the far end of the bench and observed my companion—the lack of mask shocked me, but then I realised she was only a teenager, very different to seeing a grown man flaunt his uncovered mouth. There was no anger or resentment today; I was curious about this new person. Even on the most beautiful day, I never find people on this bench, and here was someone for a second day in a row.

What is it about teenage humans that look so uncomfortable in their skin for so long? Is it that their bones have grown before their skin has time to catch up? Or am I noticing the freshness with which they hold their bodies, not weighed down by the movements of decades? I had assumed from her bent-over position that she was staring at a phone, but I was surprised to see that she was staring at her palms, or at nothing. She was bored, lost in her own world, entertaining herself with her mind in a way that I had feared teenagers today would never learn.

Eventually she noticed me and looked across, reservation and even fear writ large across her face. I remember that fear; I felt it too as a teenager. I was afraid of everything—afraid of what strangers might do to me, afraid of boys, afraid of losing friends, afraid my life would never amount to anything of worth. Looking back over my life, I have often wanted the opportunity to go back and tell the younger version of myself to not be so afraid, to reach out and take hold of all the opportunities that life would present to me. I had a sudden urge to say this to this teenager, to impart some life-changing worldly vision, but in a split moment, I thought about what I was about to say. I don't regret my teenage years, or my life choices; my life is beautiful and rich, and this happened despite my fear, or perhaps because of it. If I could somehow go back and erase the fear from the mind of my teenage self, what would that achieve? The first thing I realised it would erase was the relationship with my beloved husband, a relationship that grew slowly out of a friendship; that slowness was driven by fear but had the effect of creating a solid friendship on which our decades-long marriage and family had been built.

I looked down and noticed an ant marching slowly across the bench, holding a comically large piece of leaf over its head like a poster, a one-ant picket line, hugely passionate about who knows what. Eventually the ant reached the teenager and stopped, turned and tried another direction.

I had been staring at my palms, trying to decipher the lifelines that lightly crisscrossed my hands. Would they tell me something about what my future holds? Could they tell me if my life would end in the same terrible way that Nan's life was ending? Out of the corner of my eye, I noticed an ant walking towards me, holding a leaf above its head. The woman on the end of the bench was still studying me. What did she want? No doubt she was some entitled boomer who was about to give me grief for some imagined slight. Well, she could try; I'm just raring for a fight.

'This is a beautiful place. I love the mist,' the woman across from me surprised me with her choice of words.

I looked around, really noticing the mist for the first time. It wasn't what I had been focussing on, but now that she pointed it out, I realised how beautiful it was, swirling in front of me. It suddenly felt like I was connected to the sky, that the ethereal magic of 'up there' had descended to the ground and, for a moment, was enveloping me.

'It is nice,' I finally responded.

'Do you live around here?' the woman asked politely.

'No, I'm up visiting my grandparents. My grandmother has had a stroke; she's in a coma...'

'I'm so sorry. That is so hard. Are you okay?'

'Yeah. I guess. It's just hard watching my mum feel so sad. And Pop seems really lost. Actually, I'm feeling a bit angry with Nan. Why did she do everything for Pop? He's completely useless, can't even make himself a cup of tea.'

The woman paused at that, seeming to not know how to respond.

There was something about this interaction which was making me more open than I normally would be with a stranger. Something private about this mist; it almost felt like I was writing in my diary or talking to myself. So, I continued.

'I had to get out of the house because I was starting to feel afraid. No one in my family has been this sick before, has been... dying. It's all I can think about, and now I'm afraid Pop is going to die too, or Mum and Dad... or me.'

The woman paused again. But it seemed like she wanted to say something.

'I think it's okay to be afraid. I'm afraid at the moment, too.' She paused then and looked thoughtful for a moment before continuing. 'I think that fear can be useful. If it helps, I think you're having a very reasonable reaction to your situation. And you won't feel like this forever.'

It's always unusual to hear an adult admit they're afraid. It's like hearing them admit they've made a mistake. The old childhood hero-worshiping mindset was still casting shadows; I'm still adjusting to this new view of adults as fallible beings. It was comforting, too, to voice my fears and have them acknowledged.

That night, I danced by myself around the living room with a glass of wine in my hand. My encounter with the teenager had been lightening. Letting go of my regrets, appreciating the part my fears had played in my life was soothing. I had just accepted a huge part of myself, and the relief was palpable. I had realised something else though; I was afraid right now, and I didn't want to admit it. This invisible virus was terrifying, and I was afraid of it. And pretending that I wasn't afraid was exhausting.

My morning walk took a little longer the next day. I had woken with a pain in my hip that was no doubt due to the ill-thought-through jump the day before. There was no way I would be giving up my one outing of the day though; I would crawl to that bench if I had to. It was another cool, misty morning. The mist gently caressed my face as I hobbled slowly through it.

The bench was empty when I arrived. The disappointment I felt upon seeing my quiet space empty surprised me. A few days ago, I had seethed with rage when a stranger had encroached on this sacred space, and now I found myself hoping to find someone.

I sat with my thoughts. I watched the mist float silently, heard the birds call their morning salutations, and felt at peace until a large sigh interrupted my thoughts. My neck snapped sideways to the seat next to me where an old lady had appeared. She was in the process of straightening her back, pushing away decades of habit to lift her head and unfold her shoulders.

This woman was wearing a mask, clearly an old mask. The patterned material had faded, the material was perfectly moulded to her nose and chin. I couldn't recall seeing someone look so comfortable in a mask before. I have been wearing one for a year now, but it still feels strange.

This woman reminded me of my Nan, my special, cuddly, comforting Nan who had taught me how to knit and how to forgive. Had taught me to never go to sleep angry and to finish each day counting the things I was grateful for. Nan's death when I was a teenager had been brutal. It was my first encounter with death, and it had knocked me sideways. Seeing this woman beside me, I felt like a teenager once more, sitting with Nan at her dining table drinking tea and eating shortbread. I suddenly longed for her wisdom and her comfort.

'This is a beautiful place; I love the mist,' I began.

'Ah, yes,' the woman answered, still looking outwards towards the valley. 'The mist has a lot to teach us.'

I chewed on that for a moment, thinking how apt that statement was, given what I had learned these past few days.

The woman went on. 'The mist comes and goes. Ephemeral, ethereal. It's a good reminder to live in the now, because now is all we have.'

The mist was beginning to clear. I could see more and more trees, then the space behind the trees, then I could see the valley beyond. After a few moments, the mist had cleared completely, and I was sitting in weak sunlight, feeling its feeble warmth on my face.

When I looked over again, the older woman was gone and I was alone again, sitting on my bench, alone with my thoughts, enjoying the moment.

NASTI PESTO

DEE BARRAGRY   DUBLIN, IRELAND

Like bone on bone, the mortar and pestle. Bone in bone. She peered beyond her blanched knuckles at the oily constellation of greens and oranges in the depths of the bowl. Adjusting her grip on the pestle and with the slightest nod of subconscious satisfaction, she resumed her firm revolutions. Bone in bone. Hip in socket. Though she didn't often find cause to use it, Rachel prized this mortar and pestle. The movement and the ritual action of extraction. The material, a lightly pitted smooth clay so richly brown it was almost black, the colour of things once wrapped and buried with ceremony in peaty places. She found even the provenance of this simple equipment grounding. Hailing from her grandfather's pharmacy, it had been first a tool of daily routine and then later a curio sporadically noticed by him when enough dust had thickened on its rim. Rachel's mind reached to the portrait of him on the mantelpiece at home, pressed and pristine in three-piece tweed, one hand tucked lengthways inside the jacket as if checking on the heart that would later let him down. Thumb on a button, palm to chest, and proud among the dense glass bottles with their weighty-snug stoppers and lids. She recalled little of the man, little more than the security of perching on his long knees in her smallness, and his bewitching assortment of silky paisley pocket squares. But she found it easy and pleasurable to misremember their existences as overlapping more closely than they had.

Her bangles rang dully against the clay, the rhythm maintained with each skirting of the bowl. She paused briefly to check the time once more and to consult the recipe, one chosen for its scant ingredients and limited technical demands. With the tip of a knife, she nudged a pungent paste of garlic into the mortar and did the maths. Five hours until the girls arrived. One to finish preparing the food. Two to change the sheets and run the hoover around downstairs. Half an hour to dash out and collect a crate of recommended wines, and then time to dive in the shower and change. Her chest galloped over a fence as she pictured having her friends in her home again, having their lips on her glasses, their coats nesting on her newel post. Their stuffed holdalls in the hallway, slung aside in an ecstasy of white-flowered hugs and overenthusiastic kisses. Even after knowing each other for so long, there would be a thrilling intimacy about seeing their toothbrushes and washbags lined up on the unit by the sink, and the satisfaction of providing comfort and shelter. It would be strange to have overnight guests again, especially after not seeing each other for so long. Her bare heels drummed on the terrazzo tiles.

Teresa, Áine and Marion. How would they be around each other, and she around them? Would the hierarchy have changed? Rachel squinted at the recipe and, reaching for the jar of cashews, she prayed for the night to go well. Silence would be only marginally better than competitive vying or, worse, that non-specific chaffing between people who ought to know each other but no longer do. Remarkably, it was only in this late moment of carefully fine-dicing nuts that she let worry flare. Would they still know each other in that innate way of long-nurtured friendships? Would they all have enough to speak about after months and months of living weirdly? It had, after all, been shockingly difficult to relate to Áine's frenetic confessions by text: fantasies of childlessness, induced by school closures, and hiding out in the family bathroom where she could sag against the cistern in peace and listen to her pent-up urine splatter in a torrent of aggravation. Rachel's cheeks coloured, recalling her own irritable dismissal of her friend's messages of woe. They'd been unbearable to receive, and in the depths of loneliness, the rapid-fire strings of complaints about tending to others' needs had felt insensitive, leading her to toss her phone aside on more than one occasion. In contrast, she'd filled her days with as many online yoga classes as she could teach, aching on waking for someone or something to love and then aching all night from overtaxing her body. Guilt carved a space for itself too, the shame of thoughts so bitter she'd worried Áine would somehow taste them, out in the commuter belt many kilometres to the north. Teresa's experience had been different again; her ceramics business soared once she figured out how to move it online, and she'd maintained her steady course through mindfulness and a dogged productivity. It couldn't have hurt that she'd fallen in love and spent lockdowns welcoming a ferocious carnality that could power a kiln. Rachel knew it made no sense, but Teresa's contentment had rankled less, been less painful, than Áine's misery, perhaps because there was no competition for sympathy. Even when the relationship ended with Ignacio's return to Brazil, Teresa had been sanguine about it, managing to frame it as a sexy chapter in an unfinished novel and producing her most popular product line to date, minimalist intersecting vases with the fluid lines of limbs in love.

And then Marion. Rachel's hand went to her throat, and the juices of garlic and peppery nasturtiums wafted from her fingertips. Marion couldn't be coming this evening. Rachel knew, acknowledged, and had recorded this indisputable fact, and yet marvelled at how she managed still to neither believe nor remember. With no warning, no funeral, and no gatherings at which to miss her, the surreality of Marion's death had been absorbed by the overwhelming surreality of everything else. Engaging her midwife's pragmatism and dark sense of humour, she'd probably have found it all quite funny and cackled 'til it aggravated her claggy smoker's cough. '*What is it going to take for you to remember I'm dead?*'

Rachel startled herself with a snorty burst of laughter, envisioning Marion's lips pursed in mock offence. She seldom laughed alone, and she luxuriated in the newness of it before wiping away a hot tear and standing to survey the garden. Her pandemic project. She reminded herself to cut some flowers for the tabletops and bedside lockers. Fragrant lavender, honest cornflower, and spires of pompom alliums. When she'd asked for seeds from her friends for the birthday-that-shall-not-be-named, she'd never have guessed at the consolation the little packets would provide. Chewed up by the monotony and pointlessness of a diary devoid of human contact, the idea had been a simple one: to make something beautiful, something that would take its own natural time and her patience to evolve. Through dead weeks, she'd watched for any details of progress no matter how gradual, from the appearance of the first green pinpricks in the clay, so tiny she wasn't sure if they were the beginnings of life or flecks of decay. Rachel hadn't bothered to specify which species she desired for her bare beds. She'd been deliberately vague to reduce the pressure on her friends, asking for a single packet of flower seeds from each that would bloom in summer so that they might all enjoy them, either through photos or, in more optimistic moods, by reuniting among them. Whatever she was sent, she knew she would plant.

Teresa chose lavender and alliums. They arrived inside a lavender envelope, with an expensive-looking handmade card Rachel guessed was bought in the trendy local deli that had sprung up in a window between lockdowns and had rapidly become part of Teresa's world. The stamp had been affixed precisely equidistant from the top and right-hand margins of the envelope, and the address was written so straight it might have been done with a ruler but was more likely attributable to artistic Teresa's unerring sense of the horizon. The flowers, once grown and cut, scented Rachel's home with sweetness, and their hues perfectly complemented the sand and cloud of her walls, as Teresa had known they would.

Áine's cornflowers, no doubt recommended after consultation with Teresa, came crammed inside a puffy packet on which an address had been crossed out and replaced with Rachel's. The damaged stamp was askew and the words all in capitals. The card was a translucent notelet, from one of those sets organised people buy to be prepared. That was Áine: she'd be entirely unperturbed that the recipient might guess that between five and eleven other people would receive a clone of this card, and sure that the sentiment was in the gesture and not the object. Rachel had grimaced to imagine the reaction to Darragh or Patrick's contribution to the process. A chunky trail of red crayon began in one corner before abruptly changing direction and skidding off the front of the envelope in a mark so acute it could only have been created by a roar of expired patience from their mother.

Marion's contribution arrived in a plain business envelope, with overpaid postage. She'd have used the stamp she happened to have on her at the time, whatever its value. A garish lime-green supermarket price sticker remained shamelessly plastered across the sowing instructions on the enclosed packet. She'd never had any time for this sort of thing, though would always go along with them in her fashion with the blunt sort of kindness she applied liberally to everything. Many times, Rachel had wondered how Marion's dog Milo wasn't permanently concussed. The way Marion patted the collie's head was more akin to dribbling a basketball than stroking, but the dog welcomed her ministrations, his tongue bouncing between his wolfy lips.

The wind ruffled the massing flowers before her, setting them bobbing as their stems entangled and scattering industrious bees. Rachel closed her eyes. What was it Dad had said? He'd spotted Marion's packet on the windowsill during a garden visit and with crossed arms and the vehemence he reserved for poor horticultural choices pronounced them infernally unkillable. They featured on his hit list, somewhere near the top. Paul had added drily that it'd be only cockroaches and nasturtiums left after the apocalypse, drawing an admiring backslap from their father. 'Pee plants,' Paul added, wrinkling his nose. They weren't what Rachel would have chosen, but she'd remained loyally mute, and when she came to plant the maligned nasturtiums, she did it with the same care as the other seeds, if not the same enthusiasm.

Nasturtium. Rachel had never got to hear the word in her friend's mouth. Marion's mispronunciations were legendary, and there was no doubt that she'd have lent the flowers an unearned exoticism with her misplaced inflections and superfluous syllables. The orange flowers had run riot, creeping across the path and threatening to swamp their more polite neighbours. Marion would have been great at gardening, had she ever been inclined to do it. She was made for the honest work of tending to the world and its wounds. Her fingers had been more pastry than pianist in character, thick and strong and pale from working nights. She had hands that could cradle every size of new human, however they'd arrived. Marion once shared that she'd had the hospital's lowest number of caesarean births on her shifts, as remarked upon by her colleagues. In response Teresa teased that the poor babies were too scared to refuse to cooperate with Marion's manoeuvres. They'd all laughed, despite knowing that the statistic was more likely attributable to years of experience and professionalism. Marion had laughed along too, but Rachel felt sorry then, and now, for diminishing their friend's rare allusion to pride in herself. There could have been nobody better suited to welcoming freshly minted citizens than Marion, a looming freckled goddess capably receiving the slippery innocent while itching for her smoke break. When she said things would be fine, everyone tended to believe her, such was the power of her comfort.

The wind chimes spun, tinkling in the wind, and Rachel's eyes and mind refocused on the present. The nasturtiums glowed under the full afternoon sun, positively nuclear and audacious below their spindlier bedfellows. She turned her attention to the pesto experiment and, with a spoon, coaxed it into a dish she'd bought on a retreat holiday in Portugal. It was through chance that Rachel learned of the edible potential of her 'pee plants.' As soon as she spotted the recipe for 'Nasti Pesto' Rachel had bookmarked it, thinking of this eventual reunion with her friends. She sniffed the unctuous mixture and took up a hefty pinch of fresh nasturtium petals to scatter artfully on the top as per the picture in the recipe. She craved intensely a moment of Marion's presence or the promise of it, her face at the front window a second after pressing the bell, too impatient for reconnection to wait on the doorstep. The suedey petals weighed nothing appreciable. Rachel released them and watched them fall like festival confetti into the bowl, a small rain of joy. A single petal missed its target and landed among the spills and fragments on the chopping board. Flower and food. She brought the unfulfilled petal to her lips and placed it on her tongue, where it sat like communion for a respectful moment. And as she swallowed it, she imagined its orangeness in the dark, making its way past her throat and its backlog of words, and her heart and its hunger. Down it would drift to the wick, to light her belly like a votive with the essence of endurance and the strength of someone stronger. Marion would be here, tonight.

TOGETHER & APART

FRAGILE MOMENTS

HELEN DOSEDEL MINNESOTA, US

Do you remember,
Those small, floral tea sets
We played with as kids?
Their delicate structure
Forcing us kids to learn
How to handle fragile things.
This small necessity—
Born from caring for things
Weaker than ourselves.
Traveled to adulthood
Like those movies—
Where the red, blue wires
Connect a ticking bomb.
Our wobbly hands,
Infected with maturity,
Are expected to determine
The correct repercussion.
Except when the teapot broke,
Existence went on, as normal.

THE STITCHING CIRCLE

JOSIANE SMITH   LONDON, UK

FOOD

Sweet bread dipped in rooibos tea
Peanuts and rye shared around in coffee mugs
Wet grapes and apple slices on kitchen roll and paper plates.
Rich, dark chocolate / like mud on the tongue.
Crumbs of home-baked butter biscuits
like offcuts / smudging the floor / sticking to fingertips
punctured by needle tips,
sewing in circles.

ALL WOMEN CARRY PAIN

A group of us on the floor / backs against the walls, hear
    the opening statement
All women carry pain—it breaks through that way
like how we cross-stitch over ourselves:
‘*We women must come together to transmit love
and not pain, and that is why we are here today.*’
We nod, and later, when ours runs low, we ask for more thread
and each woman stops her work / to stretch / and cut / and
    pass a metre along,
so that the work of her neighbour can begin again.

THE BREASTFEEDING WOMEN

Two women, new mothers, strangers but for these four walls
spill out over their swollen breasts /
admit to feeding babies that don't latch, through gritted teeth /
    no milk / nipple pain.
One describes the long nights of leaning / into a pump, which
    whirrs and stirs
the squishy woman out of her.
‘*It turns me into a robot*’, and she bows her head.
A knowing woman tells her, ‘*lie back, relax into it; it will come*’

to which they both seem relieved, breathe, laugh even
and their eyes sparkle / there are some things robots cannot do.

THE EMBODIED WOMAN

The sciatic nerve is the longest running nerve in the
        entire human body.
When it is under pressure, it flares
nothing can continue / it is devouring.
She clicks her tongue at the messy underside of my cloth.
I'm eager for her approval as she tries to show me the learned way,
when suddenly her face puckers,
sucks air through a pale mouth.
The stool loses its use / the stick offers no remorse.
Radiating pain / doubles her / into false submission:
nowhere is a resting place for an embodied woman.
But storyteller and poet knows how to
gather others and make them still / at her feet. So I just watch
        as she
unpicks the threads of herself /
and awaits relief.

NINA SIMONE

When we are quiet, concentrated on finishing the stitch,
the voice of Nina Simone lifts our silence / out of the shadows.
One woman met her once,
watched her being interviewed
by some white man who wasn't dazzled by that much soul /
        didn't know god
when he met her.
Nina had been offended that
this man
didn't seem to know who she was.
So it seems, even gods are bruised by disregard.

THE HEARTBREAKS

'Tell me the formula to keep a man,'
I hear one woman ask, and I laugh.
'They want a woman, not her spirit.'
'They made me think the problem was with me.' I stop laughing
and start stitching / forwards / stitching / forwards.
Thread knots, double hems.
Try not to think about the men I left in England / dumped
      in the archives.
Tears pool in my eyes.
I can't help but match my own sorry cases to the heartbreaks
      of these women
across four countries and three decades:
there's a sadness and solidarity both,
in witnessing how we've all been ill-loved just the same.

THE THREAD SPOKE

Then the thread said,
This is enough.
I am tired.
So we bundled up the patches of rough cloth
to which we had all been faithfully adding borders.
We are told that each piece makes a whole, that makes a story.
The audience only see one side,
but *'I am an artist, and I see another.'*

And so it is.
Somewhere in the messy middle,
the stitching circle was where
the work had been done.

TWIN TUB

MAX RIDDINGTON   DORSET, UK

Jimmy had brought something back for her. Being a travelling salesman had its perks, and he was going places in the firm. The Board loved a family man.

'You know how hard he works,' Jane explained to her mother, when she asked her to take the baby overnight again.

Jane's mother nodded.

'You look a little peaky love, are you eating enough meat?'

Jane had been on the grapefruit diet for a fortnight, a slice of grapefruit with every meal. She heard about it at the hairdressers, how the enzymes in the fruit help to break down fat.

'You lose ten pounds in ten days,' said the junior washing her hair, the only ounce of fat visible on her body was her plump lips.

Day fourteen, and Jane had gained two pounds, a profound hatred of grapefruit and was seriously looking for another hairdresser.

'I'm fine mum. Baby tired that's all. You know.' The words dropped from her mouth like an irresponsible teenager tumbling out of bed.

Jane was her eldest, blonde as a summer's day and smiley with it but she hadn't always been her only child.

Life was defined by before and after the accident. If only her husband and baby son had stopped to buy an ice cream, tie a shoe, pop into the library. A few more seconds was all they needed to be in the right place at the right time.

Over the desperate days and nights that followed, Jane's mother wanted to join her men in the other world. It was only the small acts of everyday life her remaining child demanded which kept her tethered to this one.

She found courage as deep as the memories she breathed. She talked to reporters, councillors, anyone who would listen and take a picture of Jane with a photo of her much-missed daddy and chubby-cheeked brother on a ribbon around her neck.

Their memorial was a new zebra crossing on a dangerous stretch of the South Circular. She cut the ribbon, looked sad for the camera and never set foot there for the rest of her life.

Jimmy called her 'mother' these days, said she hadn't lost a daughter but gained a son. Jane flinched but said it really was an act of kindness.

Jane's mother wasn't so sure. Jimmy may be able to smooth-talk his customers, but he was as selfish as the day is long. She wished her only child had married a man who loved her as much as himself.

She had found travel brochures and a letter about the company opening a new office in Sydney last time she babysat. Jane's mother couldn't sleep for a week after that. She watched Alan Whicker's program about Australia and got a book from the library. You mustn't believe everything you see or read, so she spoke to some of her knitting group who had family out there.

'It's so hot they eat Christmas dinner on the beach,' said a woman finishing a balaclava. 'I'm not sure a roast potato is made for that climate.'

'Lots of sheep,' said a newcomer expertly navigating a cable knit sweater.

As she poured the tea, Jane's mother made up her own mind about the land Down Under.

It was ten thousand miles away.

Jimmy was glad to be home. Staying in digs all week was fine, the bacon crispy and his landlady attentive to his every need (what happens on the road, stays on the road).

But he missed sweet, compliant Jane. She may have become a little melancholic since the baby arrived, but nothing those happy pills couldn't deal with.

He removed his driving gloves with surgical precision, noted down his mileage in the company logbook, then marched up the drive with the confidence of a semi-detached homeowner. The prospect of an entire weekend washing and waxing the new company car made him glad to be alive.

'I'm back Janey!' Jim announced, reaching for his suede slippers waiting by the door like a pair of dutiful labradors.

Jane adjusted the new bra, which lifted and separated she wasn't sure what, and ran downstairs to greet him, breathing in to conceal the extra grapefruit pounds.

They pecked each other's cheeks. Jimmy wiped Jane away, even though she left no lipstick smudge.

'For you,' he said handing over a large cardboard box, gently ushering her towards the kitchen.

'Jimmy, I didn't mean for you to actually get the...'

'First things first,' he said, already impatient.

She put the box down on the counter and fetched Jimmy a cold beer from the fridge.

'Open it,' he said.

She took the bottle opener from his hand and flipped the metal top. The beer sighed with relief, unlike Jane.

He laughed at her. 'The box, stupid.'

'Sorry.' Her hands shook as she carefully pulled back the packaging. Then, Jane let out a blood curdling scream.

'Shhhh! The Moffats will hear and we don't want a repeat of last time.' Jimmy put his hand over Jane's mouth and took a large swig of beer

Jane couldn't breathe and started to panic.

'No need to get hysterical,' he said, removing his hand from her face. The mark would fade. 'It won't bite.' He lifted the lobster aloft like a prized golf trophy. 'It's all taped up, look.'

Jane had lost the feeling in her legs too.

'Pull yourself together. Honestly Jane, you're a grown woman, a mother for god's sake. All this carrying on has to stop. That lobster needs to boil, pronto before we both get food poisoning.'

'It's alive!' she stuttered.

'What d'ya know, they come that way.' He took another beer from the fridge.

'Now hurry up and cook it. I'm hungry and frankly bored with all the amateur dramatics. I've had a busy week.'

Jane peered around the kitchen for a suitable implement with which to render a lobster unconscious.

'Can't you at least stun it or something?'

'Won't feel a thing,' he called from the lounge to the sound of the six o'clock news.

Jane doubted that was true; she watched Jacques Cousteau. 'I don't have a big enough pot,' she said to herself and the lobster.

Not that she could kill anything. All of God's creatures that made their way into Jane's world were released back into suburbia significantly better nourished and cared for than when they arrived.

She sat on the cool lino floor and worried what to do next and then about what would happen next. He'd already had a couple of beers on an empty stomach. She'd hidden the scotch in the baby's pram—he'd never look there—but there was still half a bottle of vodka in the cabinet. She hadn't dared touch that; it would be too obvious.

Suddenly Jimmy reappeared, red-faced, tie undone. He dragged the twin-tub washing machine across the kitchen floor into position next to the sink, where it sat like a convalescing patient on an unexpected outing.

He put the lobster in the machine without a word.

She had a love–hate relationship with that twin tub. Whilst it saved her handwashing the baby's terry nappies, the fact it had arrived on Valentine's Day, well, she hadn't quite come to terms with that moment of wedded bliss.

'I don't know what to say Jimmy,' she told him over their romantic boil in the bag supper. 'I've never had a washing machine as a Valentine's present before.'

'You can thank me later,' he said, squeezing her breast as if checking the rise on a newly baked loaf.

Every day leading up to Valentine's Day, she had paused at the florist's window on the shopping parade and admired the display of roses, their long stems a crimson forest. Sometimes, she'd park the pram and dash inside, simply to inhale the intoxicating perfume.

'Soon be the day for lovers,' the florist said.

Jane nodded. Imagine, a husband who gave you roses.

Today, her husband was the bearer of lobster. God knows how long that poor thing had been trussed up, travelling down the M1 at precisely 69 mph to the sound of Roger Whittaker.

'All yours darling, fill her up.' He plugged in the machine and tapped his watch. 'Supper on the table by the time I've had my bath. We'd better not have run out of my bath salts either.'

Jane forced a smile.

Alone, she peered into the depths of the washing machine at the helpless creature. Its seabed was now nappy fluff, a stray shirt button and a floppy piece of elastic from a pair of Y-fronts that had seen better days.

She recalled how a crustacean's shell sheds when pressure builds, so it burrows under a rock for protection, vulnerable until renewed.

It certainly wasn't meant to end its days in a twin tub in Acorn Close.

Jane poured a glass of cold water and automatically reached for her pills. She tipped a green-and-red torpedo into the palm of her hand, like she'd done so many times before.

This time, she put it back in the bottle, found the kitchen scissors and carefully cut off the bands confining the lobster's claws. It didn't move. Maybe it was already dead. She couldn't boil it either way.

Jane had never eaten lobster. Never wanted to. Unlike Jimmy, who insisted they were an aphrodisiac.

'Isn't that oysters?' Jane said.

'All shellfish,' Jimmy declared. 'Seafood and… eat it!'

Did she really used to laugh at his jokes?

They met on holiday. He was a few years older, had a car, an old Mini that wouldn't start in the rain. They kissed under the pier, had chips under the stars and brief underwhelming sex down a country lane in the back of the broken-down Mini. By the end of summer, she had abandoned her dream of becoming a nurse, enrolled in a typing course and announced their forthcoming marriage.

'The registry office?' her mother had said.

'Jimmy thinks big weddings are a waste of money.' Jane filled the kettle, the disappointment on her mother's face obliterated by the steam.

'But what would your father say?'

Before Jane could repeat her rehearsed answer, the potato peeler fell from her mother's hand as if she'd mistakenly shot someone. 'You're not, are you?'

Jane gently poured the glass of water over the lobster and watched its shell glisten underneath the kitchen's florescent strip light.

She reached down into the drum of the twin tub, held her breath and explored, as if searching for lost treasure.

Her long fingers met smooth shell and a surprising sense of calm.

Upstairs, Jimmy had just started his Matt Monro repertoire. It was now or never.

She put the lobster back in the box, and to her delight, it managed a sickly wave of approval. Proof of life. She kicked off her high heels, found her flats and grabbed the car keys from the telephone table.

She'd had a few lessons before the new rule about wives not driving company cars was introduced and read *The Highway Code*, cover to cover, in the library while the baby slept.

She waited for the bathroom crescendo, then opened the front door.

Outside, the Moffats were off to their weekly rehearsal of *The King and I*.

They waved, and their tandem bicycle did a slight jelly wobble.

'I didn't know Jane had passed her test,' Jane heard Mr Moffat say to his wife. 'Are you sure you're pedalling, dear. The hill's coming up.'

Jane threw the driving gloves into the passenger well and put the box on the seat beside her. 'I can do this,' she said. The lobster shuffled in agreement.

The key caught on her first try, and the engine purred. 'More gas' she said, mimicking her driving instructor. Then she added his favourite phrase: 'Power to the people.'

Gears crunched, and Jane kangaroo-hopped the car onto the road.

Jane's skin tingled all over. The coast really wasn't that far away.

At the end of the cul-de-sac, Jane caught a glimpse in the rear-view mirror of Jimmy half-naked, arms waving, a bath towel precariously close to slipping down to his ankles.

She pressed her foot firmly to the floor and accelerated into the dark, salty night.

MOP WALKS INTO A BAR

RYLAN RAFFERTY   LOS ANGELES, CALIFORNIA, US

Casual. Easy. Chatting. Drinking. We talked about work, shared home improvement projects, and exchanged personal motivation hacks. "How nice it is to have friends around with similar goals and interests," we said. We had worked together on a job a few months back and kept meaning to catch up. Hang out. *Casual.* A few new book suggestions and two margaritas later, we closed our tabs and called it a—

"This is a date, right?"

Wait. Suddenly I wanted to run, but my legs felt stiff, wooden. An otherwise considerate question, his tone made it sound like a cute joke to ask something so obvious. How could I handle this in a way that I could still collect my prize: a genuine and friendly, "Let's do this again sometime."?

I retraced the night in my mind: what signals had I sent? *Catch up. Hang out.* It didn't sound like a date. The bar we chose was in a bad part of town. I bought my own drink. I pulled out my own chair. He never asked if I was single. We both wore wrinkled T-shirts. No flirty banter. In fact, he went on for twenty minutes about his new obsession with Dickens's ideas on social justice and morality. Fine conversation, but far from seduction. The answer to his question was obvious to me, but my compelling body of evidence meant nothing, as it carried the unintentional consequence of questioning his romantic prowess. My brain was spinning, but my face was frozen. He raised an eyebrow impatiently.

"No, I don't think so." I tried to keep my voice casual and friendly.

The warm person with whom I'd just shared an evening of laughter, empathy, and support had in a single moment died, never to be seen again. "So, what was this then?"

What was this then?

His icy stare reminded me of a book I'd read about black holes, vacuuming up matter regardless of size, material, or feelings. A natural disaster too primitive to value personhood. There was no begging or bribing a black hole. They consumed and annihilated.

I tried reasoning anyway. "Well," I said. "*Friends* are people who connect—"

He chuckled lightly. "People? You're not a person. You're a mop."

What? Was that some sort of archaic euphemism I didn't know because I hadn't read Dickens?

I caught my reflection in his empty pint glass: I was indeed a mop. White, synthetic dreadlocks draped over my metal face, fastened to a stick by flimsy screws and super glue.

"Why would I come all the way out here to meet with you if I can't take you home to wash my floors?"

Suddenly, we stood face to face in a department store, the bar patrons now browsing through cleaning supplies. I'd inconvenienced a shopper.

Gym Rat: "He's a nice guy. I can't believe you led him on like that."

Vanilla Mom: "What are you? Like, a knockoff brand? You don't even deserve him."

Bored Housewife: "*Au contraire!* She's designed for smooth gliding and shine. He has hardwood. It's a match made in heaven."

The Bartender (now Floor Supervisor): "I'm sorry, sir, I'll get this mop recalled right away." He dialed the recall hotline as I perspired through my moisture-lock ringlets. This was bad.

I had decent balance on my handle so I speed-hopped toward the door, narrowly avoiding hostile hands groping for my capture.

"I'm not a mop! I'm a person!" I yelled to everyone, including myself.

He scoffed, clearly the winner in the war I'd waged on his virility. As I bobbed up and down through the aisles, I could hear him echoing through the store speakers:

"Who's pathetic now, huh? Not me!"

Third floor.

"You think I'm gonna chase after you like some lost puppy my whole life while you feel sorry for me?"

Second floor.

"I was just doing you a favor! *I* feel sorry for *you!*"

Automatic doors in sight.

The Recallers waited outside. Their truck bed overflowed with various broom guts, cracked dust pans, and yes, disemboweled mops—my near future if I conceded.

With a jolt of adrenaline pulsing through my fast-acting sponge-brain, I flung the metal part of my head underneath the boot of the

Recaller closest to me, and as he stepped, my body swung upward, my handle hitting him in the face. His human skull bounced backward into his associate's nose, buying me time to dive into a tall bush nearby.

From the building to my left, I overheard a breaking news report: "Next up, there's a mop on the run. Beware, as it's been diagnosed with delusions of grandeur after rejecting a valued local shopper. Safely in the care of friends and family, the shopper's ego is expected to make a full recovery from the savage encounter."

Should I have gone home with him? Maybe I could've just quickly cleaned his floors, since I bet he sincerely thought I would. We seemed to get along, after all. Maybe even a long-term commitment could work. Plus, my options were limited since a lot of people already have mops at this age. And even if I couldn't clean as thoroughly or efficiently as he'd hoped, perhaps I could just be a good mop until he found a great mop and then we would naturally slip into being casual hangout buddies who don't clean together anymore.

But none of that mattered, because the moment for a friendship had passed. And then I realized the moment hadn't passed at all—it was never there. In his eyes I was always, and would only ever be, a mop.

Great revelation, but contemplating my value had given the Recallers time to recover and locate my shrubby refuge. There was no escape. They snatched my handle and dismantled my frame with decisive muscle memory, tossing me piece by piece into the bed of the truck. The pain seared through every lost limb before settling into phantom aches. As we traveled to the junkyard, I looked up at the stars who hadn't fallen prey to black holes, feeling fortunate to be there instead of sitting paralyzed in the moment just after he'd said, "*So, what was this then?*"

But that was just a wish, because I was still in that moment, still at the bar. An apology bubbled up my throat, eager to disinfect the stain on our evening. But he was not a black hole, and I was not a mop.

"This was friendship. Let's do it again sometime."

GENDER INEQUALITY ON 19TH-CENTURY MINNESOTA FARMLAND

JONATHAN GREENHAUSE   JERSEY CITY, NJ, US

I know too little about cows & milk curdling, about how much manure
will cause cabbage to flourish. I'm only certain

the crap I'm producing isn't the right kind of fertilizer for verses
to sprout wings, to glide towards a Midwestern sun;

so I scrape dull metaphors from the page, this auto wreck of syllables,
like clearing an 18-car pileup. Beside me,

my 5-year-old stares at an *Elephant & Piggie* book, is a perfect mix
of self-absorbed & despondent; I put pen aside,

teach him to focus on the uncharted roads bending between letters.
It's not a giving up of my poem, just

a suspension, a recognition that our time here is limited: At lunch,
I'd written about this, absentmindedly

deserting it on the table, where a squirrel grasped the paper & fled.
I muse about cheddar, about Scandinavian wagons

racing Westward & settling into geometric plots, bodies buried there,
as I bear my sleeping son to bed, free the sheets

of his stuffed animals, make room for his dreams to form. To the side,
I spot the poem my son had squirreled away:

Scanning the lines, it's perhaps the finest thing I've ever written;
but then, a thought pops up: What's the point

of writing anything else? My wife, half-asleep, asks what's wrong,
reads my poem, then lovingly whispers:

"Don't worry, it's not that good."

THE OCEAN

MAILE JUAREZ   TROY, NY, US

Sometimes I go out to the ocean in January.

I pull my plain wool coat tight and trudge through the sand dunes toward the gray waves. Everything is gray—my hair, my coat, the waves, the sky, the thick fog. Even the smooth, wet sand is gray, reflecting the faint light of the sun behind the clouds. I lay out my cotton blanket on the sand, a few yards out from the thin foam. The wind is so harsh that its pummeling almost drowns out the crashing waves and crying gulls. I imagine my curly gray hair floating on the breeze, but I know it is whipping about me, erratic and wild, like it's caught in a hurricane.

I am alone.

I was alone.

Electrical engineering in the late seventies was a boys' club, and I was the only girl in my college classes. Most of the boys were okay, but I wasn't like them. They talked differently when I was around, like they had to be careful. I wasn't one of them. Most of them weren't misogynists, but it seemed like every semester someone would say something.

I wore gray T-shirts, plain blue jeans, wide-rimmed glasses, and my curly hair in a low ponytail so I wouldn't stand out, but all my professors called on me. I learned to always read before class so I wouldn't make a fool of myself when they made me stand up.

"They'll pick on you in industry, Dana," Dr Reynolds told me, peering from behind wide-rimmed glasses just like mine. "I don't call on you because I want to embarrass you. I want you to get used to it."

"I don't want to have to get used to this," I said.

"Then drop out. No one's making you stay."

I stand up and walk out to the waves. It's already cold out here, but I take my old sandals off and slowly tread down to the foam. I let the waves lick my feet. The first time, it sends a chill through my legs. My feet are in shock, and it is so stingingly cold that I want to run back to my blanket, wrap myself up, and stay away forever. But, perhaps against my better judgment, I stay, because I love the ocean. I let my feet sink into the sand; I let the waves engulf my toes, and slowly, eventually, my feet become numb to the pain.

I feel nothing as I stand there, squinting out at the ocean, gulls diving into the crashing waves, wind whipping at my wool coat.

Dr Reynolds got me my first job.

It was at an electrical contracting company, and the salary was sixty-five thousand dollars, unheard of at the time. The boys in my graduating class said I only got it because I was a girl, but I doubted they had a 3.9 GPA and a professor with a vast web of industry connections behind them.

Then, on my first day, my new boss put his hand on my thigh.

I told my girlfriend at the time, Alicia, and she said I should quit.

I wanted to listen to her, but I couldn't turn down sixty-five thousand dollars.

My boss, Mr Anderson, used to come to my desk while I was working. He stood behind me, so close I could smell his fetid cologne, and I knew what he was doing. I started wearing turtlenecks, even in summer.

"You need to tell him to stop." Alicia looked earnest, her black hair tucked behind her ears.

I had told her about the staring. About coming up and giving me shoulder massages and saying I should return the favor sometime. About the jokes that we both knew weren't really jokes.

And I told her about how he wasn't the only one.

"What if I get fired?" I asked.

"Dana, you could get a job anywhere. You were the best in your year."

"What if everywhere is like this?"

"Then maybe you shouldn't be an electrical engineer."

But I loved electrical engineering.

I couldn't leave. I stayed, and I got used to it. I was actually very good at ignoring it.

There is a difference between standing in a thin layer of January ocean water and getting tackled by a January wave. I am standing there for so long that my feet have become entrained in the sand, and I am caught off guard when a massive wave appears. I am too stuck to run away, and as it engulfs my knees, I topple into the freezing water. I scream. Everything stings.

I cannot get used to this. I grab my blanket and trudge home. As I walk, my whole body burns from the cold.

I had worked at the company for two years, and I was up for a promotion. All of my male colleagues who started at the same time had already been promoted, and Alicia gave me the bravery to ask for myself. I had worked as hard as any of them, if not harder, she told me, and certainly been through more.

Mr Anderson asked me to close the door when I entered his office. His desk faced the door, but he told me to pull the seat around behind the desk so we could talk face-to-face. The desk was between me and the door.

There are some things too big to ignore.

The memory of the cold is enough to keep me away from the ocean for months. I can't forget the way it stung, or how long I had to sit by the heater to recover. My wife, Alicia, makes me a cup of coffee with beans our son, Brandon, sent us from college. She has always been there for me.

It's not until April that I finally decide to go back. It's a warm day, and I have missed the ocean. I sit out by the water, now knowing better than to put my toes in, and listen, and smell the beach. I *have* missed this. I can enjoy the ocean without entering the waves.

But then it starts raining.

I'm not ready for this, but I am determined to endure it, because it really has been a long time since I've been to the ocean and I really have missed it, and rain might be annoying, but at least it isn't cold.

After I quit my job, Alicia and I bought a café by the ocean on the East Coast, far away from our parents so they wouldn't ask questions.

We'd run that café for decades when Dr Reynolds called me. It was a few months after 9/11. He wanted me to take on a position in the Electrical Engineering Department.

"I have a life out here," I said. I almost said, "and a wife", but Alicia and I weren't actually married.

"This department has gone to shit," he told me. His voice was gravelly now—he must have been almost seventy. "I need someone on my side."

"I can't stand office politics."

But Alicia and I talked it over. She missed her family. I cared less what my parents thought now than I had when I was twenty-two, so being close to them wasn't as terrifying. And I missed engineering.

We went back.

Alicia bought a new café, a quirky place on the coast. I drove half an hour to work to be a lab instructor.

Being a faculty member was hard.

I was the only woman, again. I got talked over at department meetings, and my student reviews were full of boys making rude comments about my appearance or voice or how they couldn't take me seriously. I cried on my way home from work. I never used to do that when I worked at the café.

But at least it wasn't like my first job. And I was so glad to be doing EE again.

It's June.

To celebrate the end of the school year, my coworkers in the EE department at the college I work at are going to the ocean. I invite my old professor, Dr Reynolds, who retired ten years ago. I always invite him to these things. I get along well with my peers nowadays, but he will always be my best friend. He's been with me since the beginning.

My red Hawaiian shirt flaps in the gentle breeze. We sit on a bright blue blanket on the sand while some of the other faculty members flirt with the ocean. It's frothy and playful today, full of vibrant blues and greens, but I am not even tempted. I lean my head on Alicia's shoulder. I am happy where I am.

INDECENT DEFEAT

BOB TOPPING   KCORALBYN, QLD, AUS

Sore-eyed, the cat man woke, as he did every morning, to the scuffle of cats from under his bed. He rolled on one side and scratched his scalp. It was after nine, and the room was stifling hot.

Through the sliding window above the bed, he could hear the ping of expanding metal. He knew the old machinery would be roasting in the yard. Weeks ago, he covered some of the old drums and parts of dissembled cars with iron sheets dragged from the shed. By now, the little shade would be devoured by the morning sun.

He raised his head and looked outside. Brown grass. Grey dirt. Iron sheets lay scattered across the ground like spent, playing cards. There were no cockatoos in sight, and that gave him small pleasure to rise a little further. A cat jumped and stretched across his leg.

'I know what you are thinking,' said the cat with the greenest of eyes. 'You want to rest.'

He rose and trawled about the kitchen in a sleepy daze. The ceiling fan snored. Sullen company this morning, the cats sprawled at random around the room, on the chairs, hardly stirring. They knew when to speak, when to keep their place. The cat man plonked himself in the sweat of his kitchen armchair, pushed himself up and found his way to the kitchen sink. He swiped at a black-faced cat basking near the plates.

'Wipe our bowls and rinse them first.' It leered.

The cat man watched the drops of water fill the jug. The pump for the water tank was broken, and gravity drained the near-empty pipes. The sink smelled of curdled milk. He air-toed a cat near his feet. Orange-striped, stumpy-tailed with one closed eye, it sloped away. In the top corner of the kitchen, a hornet had left a hard mud nest. He thought about its unneeded presence. At least a broom length's sweep if he used a chair.

'Your knees would hurt,' muttered a cat scuttling from his reach. 'It will wait until tomorrow.' The cat man scrawled a two-word reminder on a yellow sticker pad and placed it under a bottle on the sink.

'I am a witness,' purred a musky cat with peripheral vision, from behind the armchair.

'Am I getting washed of this sump-oil stickiness?' asked a cat from the top of the fridge. 'Add that to your list. Milk bowls and car machinery don't go well together.'

The cat man heard and continued to work the tap, taking his time until his cheeks were red. He paused, overcome with weariness. There were batteries to charge, a tyre to change and a car with a buckled head. Outside on the clothes line, the hoist flapped and stopped, heavy with pegged shirts, shorts, and thin cotton sheets. A steel picket stood upright by the hoist, shrouded in a longer length of black poly pipe. In the haze of the morning, much higher than the hoist, a white cockatoo hung upside down wired to the top of the post by its feet.

'Waste not,' said the dead cockatoo. 'Your cats are serial killers, and my presence deters the birds. Now they can lap their milk in peace.'

Over the thin, paling fence, perhaps thirty metres away, his elderly neighbour fed the birds from her back door. She scattered corn and wild bird mix. The cat man wondered why she wasted money on seed. She was older, by appearance, not requiring conversation, except to chastise and throw empty tins at his cats. He decided that the paling fence dividing the properties was a boundary not to be crossed.

'Thank you for that,' said the dead cockatoo. 'She protects us and despises feral cats.'

She would be inside her house out of the heat. This morning, so was the cat man. His unhurried routine began late afternoon, after sleep-ins, picking his way around the relics of cars, upturned drums and car motors resting on grey wooden pallets. From a labyrinth of tracks between stacked timber and drums, the cats crawled out. Two. Three. Four. Scrawny, corrugated bodies.

'You are among the homeless and lost,' said a cat. 'Your bits and pieces, like us, want for attention and repair.'

The cat man would let their eyes follow the bowls as he continued into the shadows of the shed and smells of spilled oil pans and grease. A feline menagerie would follow in his hobbling exit, leap in all directions, claw the boxes and drums and disappear into the long yard shadows and tall, brown grass. He would place the few milk bowls here and there, away from the far backyard fence. His legs favoured the closer spots.

By this time of the day, he would hear the birds. The crows came in first. One at a time, they would sit on the dividing fence until they tired of the cats prowling in the shadows and hiding in the grass. The cockatoos were next. He could count them if they stayed on the fence. Once her seed was scavenged, the cockatoos screeched in formations and settled on the hoist and gutters of his shed.

He was over their ritual destruction—gnawing the washing and wires of his starter motors, and upturning the milk bowls.

'There are too many for us,' complained a tabby cat.

The cat man heard the words, looked at the cat, walked slowly to the shed and kept on with his jobs. There were batteries to charge and a car with that buckled head. He looked at the car on the wooden chocks. Despite the shade from the roof, the perspiration stuck to his skin. He felt irritated. From inside the rim of an old car tyre lying in the dirt, some kittens crept out in response to his shuffling tread. He caught a strange sound. He thought he saw a white-coloured shape swoop down from the shed and looked again in the glare of the light. It was a white cockatoo flustering a black kitten near the fence. The aggression of the bird, with its raised crest and brazen stance, disturbed him. It opened its yellow beak. He looked for something to throw before it flew away.

'A persecuting bird?' chided the kitten before it jumped behind the tyres. 'Are you defending us?'

The cat man lingered, looked at the tyres and the car on chocks. He worked out how to do things. Nothing complicated. He searched in the shed until he found his chicken-wire trap. He had tried catching the crows until beaten by their craftiness. It was over a week since the last bird was replaced. He will trap another cockatoo, and tonight, he decided, he would strike.

By the last light of day, it would be silent in the neighbour's house. He would wait until the darkness closed, throw two or three handfuls of rat-bait pellet and wheat seeds towards her back door, and retreat quickly to his armchair in the kitchen before going to bed.

It was dark early, when the sun dropped behind the shed, but not dark enough. Above the house, a one-quarter moon hung in the sky like a broken plate. The dead cockatoo on the pole managed to shift its withered head. The bird saw that the lady with the seed could not sleep. It noticed her restless turns in bed, and again as her long, black shadow left her room as though to escape a persistent heat.

From the corner of a reddening eye, the bird saw another movement in the soft shadows near the shed. A cat perhaps, but not a cat. The cat man had chased and locked the cats inside his house and shed.

The cockatoo saw the lady's back door open a slit, and in the faint shadows from the fence, the cat man was miming a punch towards the door. The bird heard a rattling on the ground like tiny stones landing hard. It watched his quick escape. More sounds followed, soft as though restrained and deliberate. Quiet, concentrated sounds as though the dirt near her door was being scoured in raking sweeps. Wide, confident sweeps.

'You can't be friends,' said the cockatoo, and watched as she allowed more yellow light from the door, as she leaned against the frame, shifting her weight on the broom, waiting for a while before looking into the near darkness by the fence. Her hair daubed grey, pale in the slice of light. She was smiling.

In the house next door, in the bedroom, in spite of the heat, the cat man was asleep in his own dark shadows. He dreamt he saw the troublemaker with her seed—screeching in anguish like the birds, howling at the sky and dropping to her knees. Fitful dreams of lauding cats stayed with him all night.

'They will not be bothersome with a fresh, dead bird,' murmured a cat with contented ease, curled up near his pillow on the bed.

The day started out like any other day in the cat man's house. Eyes grained from late sleep, his breakfast shared at the kitchen table with the cats. This morning, he drank black, tepid tea with what water was left from yesterday. One lopsided cat lapped at a puddle at his feet. When he stood by the window, his eyes rested on the bright sky. He breathed heavily and stroked his chin. The heat made his skin prickly to touch. The tap dripped. There was no wind. The hoist and clothes were still. The washing looked starched in the morning's heat. At the top of the high pole, a white cockatoo hung limp, its one black eye on its own shadow on the ground. Soon, he would venture outside, waddle about on his usual rounds and lean casually over the fence to scrutinise her backyard. His head rocked slightly with anticipation.

'Look around again before you sit,' warned a cat from near the sink.

A blurred movement caught his eye in a breeze. It was at that moment, the cat man saw a white plastic bag dangling in the murky, morning shadows of the fence. The cat man felt his throat begin to tighten. An anger slowed his breath. He told himself to focus, but all he could see in his mind was the dark shape of one of his kittens twisted in the bag, dangling by a short length of fencing wire over his side of the dividing fence. One of his worldly creatures, crumpled in a bag, tied roughly and thrown back in his face.

At first, the sudden sound chilled the dead cockatoo on top of the pole. It stirred the yard.

It was more than a bawl from inside his house. It was shrill. The bird heard all of this. The glass breaking, the furniture shifting and noises like frenzied cats fleeing to shadowed corners and hidden haunts.

From its position, the bird regarded all of this. Inside the house, the cat man was slumped in a chair, his shoulders shaking, queasy as a man who had lost. An abandoned stillness returned, and the perimeter of the cat man's house and yard became peacefully quiet.

MOTHERS & FATHERS

THESE SENSORY CHANGES

JONATHAN GREENHAUSE   JERSEY CITY, NJ, US

As my father ages, his senses inevitably
intensify, his sight

a lightning round of x-rays, his hearing
picking up the dropping

of safety pins, the farts from fruit flies,
the chattering teeth

of coatless chihuahuas. His taste buds
no longer perceive anything

as bland, a bowl of white rice as piquant
as jalapeños' seedy puree,

as salty as the Dead Sea, & his nose is led
to distant gardens

by the eye-blink aperture of a single bud,
by the aromatic churning

of humus engineered by the recent birth
of an earthworm.

MESSENGER

LEONE GABRIELLE   SEYMOUR, VIC, AUS

Mum wishes to sit down. Quietly, I move dough and stacks of paper off the chair. A clutter of notes, books, more dough, pile my bed. I have to shuffle (my room) so she and I can sit. I slip a ball of dough from a seeker-finger into my mouth.

She said, 'This is why Dad's plan will change…'

My cricket alarm broke me, woke me. Right now, I'm writing up this dream—I remember a faint feeling of movement. Boat, house, rocking, and all this raw dough, piles, on my notes, on manuscripts, on paper. Why was I cooking in my bedroom? Was I? Is it that I am just making dough? Eating all of it? Dough(y) me?

Mum starts with—and I have to say, Mum is her younger self, the self that is hidden. She is long-legged, relaxed in the chair with a leaning back slant. With a loose casual confidence. A self, who, I believe, only lives inside the ice-mouse, who I know as my mum, who long ago hid her intelligence and lost her keys, who my aunty steps on. This is a long-legged 'inside' mum, talking to me in my unstable bedroom full of projects. She begins by saying, 'Do you know of so and so's two boys?'

I have a vague understanding, though I can't place them as an awake person (writing this memory).

'They bought rings, both of them.' She speaks in terms of rings they have and how their plans are, in a way, a ring trading. Then she asks, 'Did it work? Are they any better off?' Obviously, the answer hangs in a pale-blue tune of a cool, sad no.

'Nothing to show for all those rings. And your father is the same. He will change.' Meaning, will he see the light.

VANTAGE POINT

SHARMAINE GRAY   VANCOUVER, BC, CANADA

in my father's hands spin galaxies

they cluster in the folds of his palm
wink from behind the pitted orange
he holds up as the sun

familiar with mass and magma
the genesis of moons
he leans across the kitchen table
forms asteroids
founds star clusters
from cups and crusts of bread

he teaches me the speed of light
the distance from the sun to the earth
leaves the alphabet
for later teachers

my father
weaving constellations

spilling planets like seeds
into my brain

MOTHERLOVE

KYM TYZACK   LEOPOLD, VIC, AUS

It was a summer of heatwaves. People flooded the beaches. Day and night. But not Bec. She held firm.

'Nobody in their right mind goes to the beach when it's over thirty-five degrees.'

She believed you waited it out in a closed-down house, under a ceiling fan. But after a particularly hot week being shut inside with two little boys, she broke.

'Okay,' she said to Ryan. 'You win.'

Early the next morning, as a half-hearted warm breeze gently lifted their hair, Bec and Ryan lugged all their beach stuff from the house to the street, where they kept their station wagon. The repetitive clang of the front gate's drop-down latch struck a dissonant chord against the drowsy houses and low grumble of the waking town. Ollie and Jack, still dreamy, shadowed Bec and Ryan on their back-and-forth trips, throwing random stuff into the back of the car. Bec snuck most of it back to the house.

When finally on the road, their progress was slow. The stubborn heat had drawn others, zombie-like, from their beds and into their cars. All headed in the same direction. Fire service volunteers jangled collection tins at the traffic lights. Bec shivered in her air-conditioned cocoon. *Aren't they hot in those yellow coveralls?*

Most of the traffic turned south at the big roundabout but they were going west. To avoid the crowds. She peeked around her headrest to check on the boys. *Good, they're asleep.* She wriggled a little lower into her seat. She couldn't help but smile when she thought of the choked traffic heading to the popular beaches.

After an hour or so, the road was all curves. Brown paddocks had given way to grey-green bushland. Glimpses of the ocean flickered through the trees. The bush thinned out the higher they climbed. The car clung to the road which clung to the cliff. They swerved around the 'big bend', and there it was. The ocean. Bec pressed her face against the window to look down on the blue mass. Calm today. Its edges fizzing instead of crashing. She couldn't believe the colour of the water. Tried out names for the patchwork of blues—cerulean, cyan and turquoise. She lowered her sunglasses to check it wasn't some polaroid trick, but there was no trick. It had been ages since they'd been to the beach. She looked at Ryan. *He'd been right. They should have done this earlier. I'm a stick in the mud.* She turned back to the view and longed to wind down the window. To feel the salty air on her face, but she didn't want to risk waking the boys.

Ryan changed gears. Bec worried that the old station wagon wouldn't make it. They used to think their car was cool, but nobody drove long-bodied wagons anymore. Her thoughts spiraled: *How long will it last? How will we buy a better one? I should go back to full-time work.* A neat, white SUV overtook them. *Bastards.* It hugged the bends. Was one with the road. Then it was out of sight. Ryan sighed. Bec looked at him. His jaw was tight, his mouth a thin line. Bec's mind raced: *Is he blaming me for something? For the road? For not turning off with the crowds? For the car? For the heat? For our life?*

A croaky voice came from the back. 'Mum. How far now?'

Bec turned around. Ollie's face was red. His hair plastered to his cheeks and forehead. She thought: *the air conditioning mustn't be reaching the back.* She tucked away the information. *Another job to do. Quotes to get. More finessing of finances.*

'Hi ya, Ol. Good sleep?'

He rubbed his eyes. 'I'm hungry.'

Jack woke too. Crying. 'I'm hot. Mummy! I'm hot.'

Time for muesli bars and juice boxes.

The snake's small head and thin upper body swayed side to side. The rest of her was a thick copper-tiled coil. Bare feet thudded past her bolt hole. Her flickering, split tongue searched the air while fifteen slick babies slipped from her into a tangle of squirm. She stayed on alert as the glistening pile of new bodies wove and wriggled around her. Thudding rumbled above the burrow. Sand showered her and her sticky, writhing, hungry family.

'I feel sick.'

'Really, Ollie? How sick? Do we need to stop?' Bec half-hoped she could talk him out of it.

He whimpered. 'Really, Mummy. My tummy hurts bad.'

With every dip and curve in the road, she could see the juice and mushy muesli bar swirling in his little tummy. *Shit. The crowds knew what they were doing after all.*

Ryan's knuckles were about to pop. Bec imagined having to prise his hands from the steering wheel when they finally stopped. He craned his head forward in search of a safe exit. His neck, all rope. Ollie groaned. Jack mimicked him. Bec's stomach clenched. *Taking the cliff-carved road was stupid. It's all going to shit. It always does.*

'Nearly there, Ols, hold on. Nearly there,' she cooed.

Without notice, Ryan swerved into a lookout and jumped out of the car just in time to open Ollie's door. Vomit flew past him. Bec pulled Jack from his car seat. He squirmed out of her arms and ran straight to the vomit action. Bec pursued. The heat was like cling wrap. The air still. Below them, heat haze and a barely breathing sea.

'Good boy, Ollie. That feels better, doesn't it? Got any water there, Dad? He needs a drink.'

Ryan checked his vomit-splashed feet, re-adjusted his priorities and handed over his drink bottle. 'Yup, here you go, boyo.'

Ollie swigged and spat. Took in his surroundings. Swigged again. Threw the bottle to the ground and ran to the barrier at the cliff's edge. Bec followed. Hovered.

'He's obviously feeling better,' Ryan called out.

'Wish I could say the same,' mumbled Bec, out of earshot.

Ryan hoisted Jack onto his shoulders and dawdled over to them. They all examined the view. Each making their own assessment. A brown creek trickled through a narrow bush-lined valley, onto the beach. The water ran clear by the time it met the sea. The expanse of shimmering water merged with the sky at an indefinable horizon. Dots of summer-beach fun sprinkled the scene. Glumness was banished.

'Let's stay here!' yelled Ollie.

Ryan and Bec looked at each other. They'd had enough of the snaking road.

So, each of them burdened with a lazy man's load, they struggled down the cliff steps. A few steps from the bottom, the boys hurled their buckets, spades and cricket gear onto the buffalo-grass embankment and jumped onto the burning sand, running and squealing towards the water.

'Boys! Wait! Your rash vests! Sunscreen!' Bec kicked off her Birks and did the hot-sand dance to catch the boys at the edge of the water.

'Look, Mum. My feet are gone!' chortled Ollie.

'Mine too, Mummy. Look. Look!' demanded Jack.

'Oh, no! Well, looks like you're both stuck here forever.' Bec faked her best light-hearted laugh, then scanned the beach. Umbrellas and beach huts wavered in the haze. Too hot for movement or noise. People lay prone or with newspapers, hats or books over their faces. *How could they bear this heat?*

She searched for a spot to set up, but there were no sandy stretches. Just small patches between black rocks. No facilities. No other little kids—not a family beach. *They'll drown. Ryan will blame me. Everyone will blame me.* She told the boys to stay put, scrunched up the edge of her skirt and waded out to check for an undertow. *I'd be happier if there was a patrol.* She walked back to the boys and grabbed each one by the hand.

'You can swim soon. We need to set up first.' They wriggled free and ran to the cool grass of the embankment. Bec pushed her way through the heat and hot sand. One step at a time.

While Ryan and Bec struggled with the beach hut, the boys tried to scramble up the grassy bank. Ollie spotted a small hole. He used it as a foothold to propel himself to the top. Jack copied him. They wrestled until they tumbled off the edge. Then did it all again. Bec looked over. *Aren't they hot? They'll get sand in their eyes.* She held back from yelling at them. *They're having fun.*

Ryan and Bec were not having fun. She wanted to ask if he was mad at her for bringing them to this wild spot. But the heat had stolen her will to start a conversation with such a well-worn route and destination.

Meanwhile the boys tired of their jumping game.

'Mum! I'm thirsty. And hot. I wanna swim. When can we swim?'

The mess of neonates had swayed close to the little toes. Their mouths stretched open like baby birds with wavering thread-like tongues. The mother's tongue assessed the air. She was shy of crowds and usually hunted at night in this weather. But even so, now that there was a lull in movement, she left their cool haven. Her babies followed. They glided over the impacted grass until they were amongst reeds and sedge. The tall spikes barely trembled as they passed through. They slipped through cool mud at the edge of the tea-coloured creek. An edgy skink skedaddled, but a preoccupied fairy-wren continued her skipping from rock to reed. The snake struck and devoured the tiny bird. The hours-old babies wriggled through the maze of grasses, hunting froglets and gossamer-winged insects.

Bec couldn't find the sunscreen. She would have to go back to the car. *God! Those fucking steps.* But the tube was laying on the grassy embankment. *Halle-fucking-lujah.* The plastic was soft. *Will the heat have affected the cream's potency?* She heard the boys. *They've followed me. Of course they have.* She unscrewed the lid. *I really should have done this earlier.*

'Let's just get this on both of you now.'

'Nooo! Nooo!' They ran. 'Nooo! Nooo!'

Bec knew her face would be red. She lifted her damp hair from the back of her neck and held it up for a moment. Her clothes were sticky. *The boy's skin will be frying.*

'Boys! Come back here! Boys!'

But they had seen the creek and were running to it. Their pale calves turned rusty as they paddled through the tannin-stained water. Mayflies hovered; small fry darted around their toes.

Bec called out to Ryan. 'I need help with the boys!'

Nothing.

She used her hand to temper the glare as she searched the beach. *Where the hell is he? Is that him? Yep.* He was floating on the flat ocean. Feet pointed to Tasmania, zinced nose to the sky. Crying drew her back to the creek. Jack had slipped, and Ollie was dragging him from the water by his arm. *Fuck you, Ryan.*

'Boys. You need to come with me.'

She waded through the cool, shallow water, resisting the impulse to fall face-first into it. Ollie had left Jack on a rock and was trying to trace the flight of insects with his finger.

'Look, Mum! Pretty flies!'

'Yes. They are pretty, aren't they? They're called mayflies.'

Caddisfly 'Plectronemia australica' (*Polycentropodidae*), *actually.*

'C'mon, boys. We've got to go. Daddy will be wondering where we are.' She hooked Jack under her arm and grabbed Ollie's hand. 'The ocean is much nicer to swim in. Look, Daddy is already in.'

They wriggled free from her grasp and raced towards their hero. 'Daddy!'

But a ragged, raw sound stopped them in their tracks.

'STOP! Snake! Stop! Boys. Stop! Snake! Snake!'

Is that me? My sound?

Books and hats slid from faces as people sat up and twisted their heads towards the sound. Bec reminded herself of the first rule of a snake encounter: Don't run. Stand still.

She screamed again, 'Run, boys, run!'

But she stayed. Had to. The snake was in her path. It raised its head. Flattened its upper body like a cobra. *It's a copperhead* (Austrelaps superbus). *Probably a female. What's she doing out in this heat?* The snake hiss-spat at Bec from the back of her throat. Fangs. Frantic split tongue.

She held her head stiff, but her lower body thrashed about. Her belly was creamy. Wet, dark copper tiles glistened along the length of her.

Bec could hear the boys calling out to their gently bobbing father, even though her heart pounded in her ears and head. She reminded herself that copperheads didn't usually strike. That they were shy. She followed the rules now and froze. So did the snake. A standoff. A movement in the grass distracted Bec. She lowered her gaze without moving a muscle. A tangle of snakelets slithered over and around their mother. *Ah.* Her shoulders dropped a fraction. She slowed her breathing. Waited for the snake to make the first move. After a minute or so, or maybe just seconds, the snake relaxed. Her stuck-open eyes stayed focused on Bec, but Bec knew it was the snake's tongue that would 'see' her. Then, shy again, the snake dropped her head and slid away. The babies followed. Bec went to take a step, but her legs wobbled.

'Mum! Mummy.' Jack and Ollie were back. They grabbed her limp arms.

Ollie was cross. 'C'mon, Mum. We want to swim, and Dad's too far out to hear us.'

'Okay, okay. But first…' Bec took a deep breath. 'But first, you little terrors—sunscreen!'

The boys squealed and ran from her. But her body was strong again, and she ran after them. Laughed. Perhaps too loudly. People looked at her.

They got home at dusk. Their faces tight from the sun and salt. The house, which had been shuttered from the heat, was cool. The boys plodded inside. Sleepy robots. Bec stripped them off for a quick bath while Ryan microwaved some macaroni cheese. Jack fell asleep while eating.

Later, Ryan and Bec stopped by the kids' room. The boys had kicked off their sheets. Their cheeks were flushed, and the breeze from the overhead fan lifted their hair. Ryan laid his arm across Bec's shoulders. She wriggled free, mumbling something about sunburn. He walked away. She heard the fridge close. Sport blurted from the television.

She sat outside with a cup of peppermint tea. The night air was soft and warm. She ran through the day's events and thought about the snake—usually so shy. She had risked the heat and all of us humans to feed her babies. Bec cringed as she remembered screaming, 'Run!' *We both broke the rules today. What are you doing now? Leading your babies back to the creek? Their creamy bellies gliding over the warm ground until they reach the cool mud. Their tongues scanning for food. It'll be quiet down there, just the hiss of the sea and the croaking of frogs.*

She took a sip of the now cold tea. Swallowed. Longed to join the snake by the creek. To study her and her babies. To record the insects, skinks and birds they ate. To collect the snakes' shedded skins. To rent a place at the coast—just for a bit—to work from a table covered in specimens. To talk to colleagues on Zoom. To swim alone. To eat when she was hungry. Today had sparked something. She was ready after all. (Wasn't she?) They needed the money. (Didn't they?)

'Babe?'

She turned around. Ryan was a dark shadow in the doorway. 'Jack wants you. Not me. You. Won't have a bar of me.'

'No worries. I'll come in.'

DRAWN TO WATER

THE PLUNGE

SUSAN Y. HOFFMAN   MADISON, WI, US

Clouds drift like constellations over the blue-lidded bowl of Devil's Lake.
Smaller than the rest—younger, too—she perches on the boulder,
a voiceless rooster with legs splayed, neck craned forward over the edge.
It's her turn.
She can't smell the white pines behind her or the future ahead.
"Go *now*."
Not yet.
"Jump."
I am not ready.
"We'll do it together. Here, take my hand."
Her arms flail like useless wings.
Below, wet faces smugly grin up at her
as their sharklike bodies form a semi-circle.
The line of lemmings in back of her grows longer.
There is gravity in the situation.
"Hold your nose and don't scream."

REALER THAN REAL

CIARA BLUM   FINGAL HEAD, NSW, AUS

Dad says that there are versions of truth. Shades. That one person's *real* is different to another's. He says that is why we are left floating, suspended, in that fragile, transient space between what is and what is not. But if there are versions of truth, then there are versions of certain—right?

And this one is mine.

PART I: THE EDGE OF REAL

Dad forgot to close my curtains.

I am woken by a modest hue of orange, seeping through my eyelids, and this is the first thought I have. The sun is warm on my bare chest, and I realise that I have lost my blanket to the whims of sleep. It lies at my feet, twisted, like those breadsticks that Mum used to make for a treat, back when she lived with us boys. And I remember that my feet have grown over the summer, and that they are now the same size as my brother's, even though he is seven and I am five-and-a-half.

I wriggle off my mattress and swing my big feet to the ground. And my footsteps leave prints, *big* ones, with four pointy toes, and the roundest, roundest heels, and the imprints of nails—like a monster. And I can't see the shapes, but I know that they are there, and if I know it, then it is for real.

That's what Dad always says.

'How will it be, Christian?' I ask, bounding onto the end of my brother's bed.

Just like the postcard? With that big, endless blue, and that shiny, soft floor? With those thumbnail people, and their thumbnail umbrellas, stuck in the ground to say: I am here?

I bite my bottom lip.

'However you want it to be, Charlie.'

My brother pulls on a T-shirt, un-ironed, and throws two beach towels into a bag. His is yellow, his favourite colour, and mine is the faded memory of a deep, dark blue. And then it is time for breakfast.

Because it's like this.

We ran from the very middle of the country, we did. From the dust, from the hot, red dirt, all the way to the water. To the edge of the world, we ran—just me, Christian and Dad. And when Christian shows me a map, I can almost point to us, tucked up in bed on the line where brown meets blue.

Where one shade of truth meets another.

And then it is time to go.

Dad says we are going to walk the edge of the world like a tightrope. And, then, we are going to close our eyes and leap, hold our breaths and dive, deep, deep, deep down, into the blue, and let the cold water swallow us whole…

And then we will *get* it, we will: what living really feels like. It's so simple.

PART II: FALLING

Well. There's this big, hungry blue called 'the ocean', and it can't quite reach the land. It keeps trying, you know—running, running, running, then being sucked right back out. Back to square one. Dad says that life is sometimes like that. Reaching, reaching, reaching for something… getting so, so close… then falling.

Falling.

I roll the word back and forth on my tongue.

We lay down our towels on the edge of the world and run, run, run until we're floating. Not touching anything but the blue; not depending on anything solid. It's kind of like our pool back home, but bigger and busier and wavier. And it is in this moment, kicking through the endlessness, that I know for sure: this is real.

It is realer than real.

It is cool. It is alive all around me. It is real.

But, all of a sudden, it is *too* real.

And it is not until I look up, right into the sun, that I realise I have been falling.

PART III: JUST A BREATH

It's kind of funny, isn't it? You know—the way that things change. Immutable things; solid things. They start to fade, start to crumble, start to slip through your fingers… until you're not sure that they were even there to begin with. But who has the right to stipulate, to define, what is there and what is not?

And how can anything exist, and then just be gone?

I breathe in the tide.

I'm like a whale, I am. Born to swim, born to glide through the endlessness, but not born to breathe without air. Not born to swallow the waves, down, down, down, deep into my lungs, like I used to inhale the sky...

I am trapped, suspended in the blue, held by the tendrils of time—and I am kicking; I am running, and I'm strong. It's true—I am—but not *that* strong. And though it is dark, though the world grieves the memory of sunlight, I can see everything.

I can see it all.

I am three kicks away from the surface, I am. But it seems as if the firmness of it all is fading and I must pretend, with cloying panic, to understand.

But here I am. Floating on the edge of the world; on the edge of everything we know to be real. My world is made of light and dark, of deep-music, of *what exists and cannot be undone...*

And it is not until now, just a breath away from the ground, from its solidity, that I *get* it: what it means to be alive; to live; to love.

The world is silent as it presses up against me, soothing, heavy with the promise that everything will be okay. And I know with certainty that this deep heat, this deep dark, is realer than real; truer than true.

I close a fist, wet with the tide, around Dad's words; around his promise. Because *this* is the edge of the world. I just know it.

Suddenly, I am clawing through the blue, through the wet, through the cold, through the empty, through the heavy, through the light, through the dark, to the surface, *back to the edge... over the edge...*

And then my hand disappears into Dad's. It enfolds mine, tugging me through the cold, slick blue.

Warm.

My chest aches, but I am safe. I am here. I am cradled in his embrace, held tightly as the waves swirl around us. And my eyes seem to close on their own, heavy with relief; with the memory of a deep dark.

Even then, as I give in to sleep, as I blink away tears, I can see it. Even then, as I settle against his forearm, I can see it.

Even then, I can see it.

I can see it all.

It's so simple.

ROBES OF DARKEST BLUE

ALICIA SOMETIMES   MELBOURNE, VIC, AUS

You stand at the edge of waves—your frame, a cratered shipwreck
as foam & water puckers around the trims of your jeans. Everything

about the light is granular, even the seagulls are overcast. You say:
a marine animal's whole world is sound. I know what you mean. Depths

so chasmic the light can't reach them at all. Beds of oceans, absent
of sun but never singular. Below must be a procession of wildness

& richness—hydrothermal vents, mud volcanoes, vast canyons
—a plethora of growth. Sonar communication is full of bustle

I say: *this is how your darkness is embraced* as eddy, rushed sequences—
rhythms of uncertainty, tread in a turbulence of tides. Wind whips

up your hair as it covers your face. Sand, fibrous & husky, ruffles
against our skin. You sigh with a roar of a winter's afternoon, our

lungs draw in every force they can muster. Boats—trembling up
& down, completely bereft without passengers. You pause as if

this is your fault, but here's the thing: you are more than sadness
falling into the tip of the sea, more than cuts of icy wail tumbling

at our feet. You—in the jumper with holes & memories of loss
can make it out this day & jump into the next, onto passing ships

gliding over the storm. Pick up seashells, crab suits without muscle
or abandoned bottle tops. Palpitating emotions skipping like stones

on waves, rising & falling with each breath, & if they don't go far
know—the way you ride the surf of passing currents—you will

& this reef, nestling on the brim of time—tendrils of rebellious life
distilled in a daring canopy of space, will outlive every last one of us

LEVIATHAN

PAUL WEIDKNECHT   PHILLIPSBURG, NJ, US

The surf retreated, pulling the sand from around her heels, unbalancing her for a moment, but that was just fine; Juliana had made it to the ocean. When she got back home, she would describe everything about it to her friends with such confidence that no one would ever know she'd only gone in up to her shins. This would be two firsts in the past month: visiting the ocean and, of course, testifying at the trial.

Down the beach, the next wave collapsed, and a flat arm of water rushed up the slope. Sunlight angled onto the packed, wet sand, bringing up a sheen, and as the foam seeped back out to sea, the shimmer faded in a serpentine line that seemed almost mystical. Little kids, six years old or so, half her age, charged into the water, squealing, laughing, their fear as far away as her Indiana farm. Juliana inched into the oncoming wash. The water rose to her knees. She turned and smiled to her mom, who sat in a beach chair behind sunglasses and a big floppy hat, looking way too much like a tourist. Another time, in another place, she might have been a little embarrassed, but not now. Embarrassment was for people who cared about what others thought.

Juliana had seen the ocean once, but that was from a distance, in the mountains somewhere along the Washington coast. Her dad had picked her up from school, and he'd kept driving and driving, past their house, out of Indiana, the car jammed with camping equipment and canned food. Every so often, he'd look over with his sideways grin like it was a regular visitation and they were going for a burger, but all she could do was stare straight ahead at the road and think there was nothing regular about this trip. As they sat in the car three days later, watching the Pacific explode against the rocks far below, he'd said they would eventually get there, but that the time wasn't right. Now she was at a different ocean, with a different parent, and everything was right.

She'd heard about this particular beach on the news, that there had been shark attacks earlier in the summer, in waist-deep water—even less—that one swimmer died, that another lost a hand. The sharks had confused people's hands and feet with fish, somebody said. She looked down through the turbid green water and waded forward.

The water was at her waist.

People said she was brave, but a brave girl would have been able to look her dad straight in the eye when she was on the witness stand. A brave girl wouldn't have made the prosecutor ask her to raise her voice so the jury could hear what she was saying.

The water came to her neck, and every time a gentle swell rolled through, she was lifted, her toes coming off the bottom. For that moment, she believed anything could happen to her.

Juliana turned onto her back, arching. She spread her arms, brought her ankles together, and floated. Closing her eyes, she let the sun warm her face, imagining herself back at the outdoor community pool, the lifeguard stand and chain-link fence separating her from an ocean of soybean fields, daring the sharks to try anything, anything at all.

REFLECTIONS &
PATHS TO HEALING

SELF-PORTRAIT

STEPHANIE WILLIAMS-HOLMES   CHRISTCHURCH, NZ

She sits in front of the empty canvas, a paintbrush in her right hand. She swipes at the pale sea, leaving a yellow gash in its belly. Fish bones and seaweed spill out onto the floor at her feet. The room fills with rot, but she keeps going.

Another slash, a sky-blue mouth. She hears the waves cry out, spraying her face with salt and spit. Another. Green eyes cry red tears that stain her cheeks. She must keep going. Orange flames leap across the sky, melting mousy hair into pale skin, and she cleaves the sea right down through its centre.

Her hand is no longer her hand.

She closes her eyes. She has painted what resides in her lungs and awakened the crows who leap from the canvas, cawing.

'Look at your face, covered in gauze. You should bury it in the sand.' 'Look at your belly, filled with stones. You promised skin and bones.' A voice drowns them out, not a screech, a gentle whisper. 'Look how the canvas has turned into a mirror.'

She opens her eyes and falls to her knees, and the portrait collapses with her. Then she rests her forehead on the cool glass and, as though falling through a cloud, she melts into the sea.

VENETIAN GLASS

KATY MASSEY   BRIGHTON, UK

The street seethes with heat. The city's jumbled facades of stone and brick exude it. Above me, too high for shade, hosts of antique angels sigh. Crumbling curlicues of marble and plaster pulsate in this damp furnace. Dilapidated balconies sag with exhaustion. Every clock has stopped, face scorched, arms baked and twisted. Ecclesiastical bells toll out of tune as I pass, clappers warped by the disgraceful temperature.

Here, a ten-minute walk on Google Maps takes at least forty. Only two days into my trip, but to get to the famous artists' exhibition, I still have far to go and more to overcome. I trip over rude Italian dogs wandering away from their owners, duck to avoid filthy air piped out to the pavements from exorbitant restaurants, fight through tour groups meandering down San Marco's tiny passageways.

The other tourists are a horror. Almost sandwiched by their sweaty bodies, I swerve the stench of football-shirt nylon clinging to damp flesh. And all the things hanging off or sticking out—cameras, backpacks, water bottles, elbows—dodging them while avoiding the clutches of tacky Murano glass vendors.

I mean, I knew it would be busy, but this is ridiculous. And I am slowing, losing pace, too aware that I could be in my cool room, sipping the hotel's sugary iced tea. Finding body space in a sliver of shadow, I lean against a rough sandstone wall, close my eyes for a second and imagine I'm lying in air conditioning, swiping through Insta, on a bed of stretched white sheets smoothed by another woman's hands.

I am out of place here. In public, I am always a little on my guard (show me a brown woman who isn't) but this is a different level. I can't cross a piazza without some sticky-fingered toddler, doughy fist folded around a dripping gelato cone, threatening to drip it down my khaki linen trousers. The parents are worse: hard eyes crawling over my copper cheeks and afro twists, my hair and face inevitably putting me in the wrong.

I carefully curated my outfits so I could update my socials with a cruise-wear vibe, but this a teeming nursery in forty-degree heat and humidity with mosquitos. Who can look good here? My hair has frizzed up; it's puffy as a black sheep, and my cream platform clogs look ridiculous. I am trying to climb Everest in mules.

No wonder you didn't come. Can't make it, you said with a sigh, pushing a lick of your long, sensitive fringe out of your wide blue eyes. (It was work. It was urgent. Of course.) Lolling on your mid-century leather sofa, you drew your legs up in front of you defensively. But the sigh seemed heartfelt, eye contact steady and pained. I can't make it, you said again, as if you not being able to *make it* meant you couldn't face the task of rebuilding this ancient city from the canals up. As if, without you, the whole place would fall into the sea.

Tears escape my eyelids. This trip was your idea—to move our relationship to the next level, you said. I'm knocking on the door of forty… you added, leaving the rest of the sentence seductively unsaid. I thought you'd ask me to move in with you, at least. And I'd already done the groundwork, found cheap flights, scrolled through recommended hotels, found well-reviewed restaurants.

But I couldn't say this, so I said nothing. You looked at me hard, as if you wanted to absorb my hurt through your compassionate stare. Could smell, I was sure, the bitter reek of my disappointment.

It's not a good time, you said. But why don't you go? And I noticed a smile crimp the very edges of your lips. As if you knew I couldn't. That if you didn't make my reality, I wouldn't have one. So, I came anyway, to spite you. I am only stuck in this shithole because I am stubborn to prove a joyless independence.

You, though, you have turned out to be a back-seat driver.

My phone dings. As I bend forward to fish it out of my bag, I am flung around, suddenly pivoted ninety degrees on my stupid shoes. The blow to my shoulder almost knocks me off my feet. A small, round man glances impassively back at me for a second before he is lost in the crowd. I lean back again, letting more people pass, rats down a drain. I barely have the energy to raise my phone to my face. Tears threaten again. Why am I doing this? It was only one of the hoards bumping into me; he couldn't have known I would suddenly lean down. But still, for a moment, I want to sink down onto my haunches, crouch in the drain in my linen, and cry like an animal.

I take a second or two to regain purpose. Eventually, I look at my phone. 'Are you there yet? I'm EXC TED!'

You bought me the ticket for this exhibition before I left. Be my avatar, you said. I wasn't especially bothered about seeing the famous artist's work, and I told you so. But he's brought together some of his most famous pieces, you countered. He's bought a *palazzo* to put them in

(I'd never heard you accent a word like that before). It's *unmissable*, you insisted. But *you will* miss it, I thought, but did not say.

Now, I am nearly there, but what I really want is to have you beside me so we can complain and laugh at these ridiculous people. You would tell me I am a snob. But I would say there is a difference between me and this throng. I travel mindfully. Unlike the overdressed couples at the hotel, I am minimal. My small leather bag lies across my body and takes up hardly any space. Neither do I. I am slim. Even my straw hat has a narrow brim.

I garnish myself with these tiny distinctions because I cannot afford to stand out. You tell me I draw attention to myself. So I try not to. And I think I fit in. You call me your tiny, dusky goddess; my chestnut skin and dark copper hair your accessories.

But this straw hat seems to make me hotter. Shouldn't it be cooling? Not sure. Is that a thing? I would ask the socials, but you told me that when I came here, I had to turn my phone off, for once. I refused. We argued, in that way we do. You insisted, going on and on, all the while pretending not to care. I compromised, promised not to look at my feeds and to turn off alerts so I could appreciate the famous artist properly.

I wish I had agreed to turn off my phone now. I feel like you are chivvying me on. And as usual, I am not living up to expectations. I don't care about appreciating the famous artist; I don't want to see his work. But you needled, in that way you do. He's so popular/the exhibition is a blockbuster/you're staying so close/it would be silly not to. And because I thought I may be stupid for not wanting to, I gave in.

I type: 'Nearly there. Excited!' Add a smiling emoji. Press send.

And according to Maps, I am getting nearer. At least the inside of a palazzo should be cool. This morning, the receptionist at the hotel told me that the buildings here are designed to be inside out. As she explained, her liquid eyes slipped over my damp forehead, licked my glowing face, and a slick of pity oiled her voice with its polite, accented, charmingly inaccurate English. In her black cravat and burgundy silk shirt, she looked newly unwrapped, her brown bobbed hair shining like a conker. It was just her uniform, but I felt shabby standing before her.

'You know the street. In summer, we run from shade to shade. But behind the grand gates, there are cool gardens and high ceilings and floors of marble.' She almost whispered this as if it were a secret, a dirty one. But it is not cool inside the tacky hotel. Every piece of upholstery is covered in jewel-coloured velvet. Every wooden surface has sticky varnish clinging to it like molasses. I wanted to tell her this but didn't. It would've been impolite. To point out inconsistencies in the expensive illusion felt churlish. The city floats or sinks on our collusion with tricks like this.

Maps tells me I am almost at the palazzo, but I am now quite sure that I am not wanted here. The ancient paving stones press painfully back against my soles. My feet ache with rejection. But then the Palazzo comes into view, appearing quite suddenly as if hiding behind a bushel for half a millennium. It is massive, the width of five houses across its crenellated frontage. The breadth of the canal in front of it means I can take it in all at once, rare in this built-up space. By size, it could be the council buildings of a medium-sized Home Counties' town. This famous artist I'd never heard of is doing the palace up. You told me he is bringing it back to its former glory to house a permanent collection of his art. Then you dropped his complicated name again, but just too quickly for me to hear clearly. Now I understand why he might want to rescue this building.

And stood here, breathless from grandeur, I also realise why it is called a palazzo. It is a half fortress, half temple to pleasure. Its windows are small and covered with decorative iron work, while the front door is the height of two men, and at least half-a-metre deep. The façade of white marble looks freshly cleaned, and there is not an inch that is un-adorned with patterned carvings. It is anointed with flowers, vines, and wild birds. The building is like a wedding cake baked for five hundred years beneath a relentless sun. It is more than a castle; it is a *palace*; a confection which expects envious eyes. Flagrantly welcomes them.

I walk, dazed, toward the massive door, which stands ajar behind a small sandwich board bearing the famous artist's name. As I near the shadow of its portico, my handbag buzzes—another text? No, it continues. A call then. I reach in and press the button to cancel it, cancel you. I can call you back when I get my bearings before this magnificence. It's as if I am approaching an altar. To answer now would be rude.

As I slip through the open door into the marble-cool hallway, a pleasant young man with pointed features walks toward me. He smiles a greeting. I ask what I should do, now I am here. The answer is not obvious to me.

Um, look around? he replies casually, his suggestion un-barbed.

We are standing in a huge space, cool and shady, and in front of us is a waterfall of what looks like melting red-and-white wax. It fills my vision, caught in time, frozen, as it tumbles from the ceiling, seemingly without a source. I am gaping at the shiny deluge. Is it wax, or is it once-liquid flesh, now solid and caught mid-cascade? I reach out a hand, but as it closes in on the sculpture, the young man interrupts.

Everyone wants to touch it, he says gently. Isn't it marvellous? It's made of silicon and canvas. His gaze joins mine in wonder, discretely giving me time to withdraw my hand. I do so, but with difficulty, despite his censoring presence. The urge to feel the falling matter, this proof of life, against my fingertips is almost irresistible.

My bag vibrates yet again, pulling me out of the moment. I have an electronic ticket, I tell the young man who still hovers. He has not asked, but I am on the point of pulling my phone out now. I need something to do, something to distract me. The sculpture, if that is how to describe it, somehow occupies me internally and externally both at once. It is too much. I am possessed. I want—am relieved—to have an excuse to look away from it, busy myself in my bag. But the young man shows me his palms and shrugs. It's okay, he tells me and lightly pats my arm, stilling it. If you have made it all the way up here, I believe you, he adds, laughing a short, light sound. He drifts elegantly away, leaving me in confusion. I expect he knows that I am going through a kind of shock. He'll have experienced this before and knows I am unmoored, struggling to repossess myself. That I am lost in the torrent of emotion running down the palace walls. It fills me up, flowing from the top of the building, through the atrium where I stand, leaking into my parched soul, dashing me into pieces in its current.

Eventually, I manage to look away. I take in the airy, newly plastered space, the small sprinkling of other visitors, the view of what looks like a small municipal park from the palazzo's rear windows. The swings and benches in the small green square don't fit. It is not wrong, just less. Surely it was once a palace garden, teeming with fountains, peacocks, and figs?

I am myself again, but not myself. I am changed, lighter. The famous artist has performed a miracle. He, with his marble palace and the paint and silicon of his torrential work, has pulled an instinct out of me. In front of this absent magician, this showman, I became a baby again, responding purely to stimuli. Because of him, and just for a moment, I knew abandon. So lost am I in this realisation that it takes me a while to notice the vibrations of my phone against my hip.

But now I want more, want to drink in the enormous space of what may have been a ballroom (might be again. Who knows what is possible?). So I finally reach into my bag and find my phone. I carefully draw it out, making sure not to read the number of waiting messages. I look away as I keep my thumb down on the home button until I am sure it is off.

I arrived alone, and I will stay that way. To experience more of the artist's conjuring without your help. And the rest of the exhibition, at least. And then, what more? I have two more days, and I am all at once anxious to feel fractured from myself again. To drown in novelty. I shall take my time here first though. The rest of the blazing city will wait for me, naked under the smouldering sun.

WHEN WINTER WENT

HANNAH BROWN   TOKYO, JAPAN

It was winter when the shadow came.

The kitchen was warm and burbling. The chicken roasting in the oven filled the room with mouth-watering scents of onions and thyme. Steam touched the windowpanes and ran down in little rivers. The house was quiet and absent, the only sounds, the sounds of cooking.

Ally was slicing up potatoes at the sink, her hands stinging, when she looked up and saw it. It stood under the swing; one hand stretched out at an odd angle to hold the rope. She'd fallen off that same swing as a child and broken her arm. Worn a bright pink cast covered in love for a while too. Now the swing seemed wrong and the thing holding it worse. Dark and shadowy and iniquitous, like the air around it was pulling itself back from touching it.

Ally's hand tightened around the knife, seized with a sudden unknowable certainty. She couldn't let Danny see it. She wasn't even sure what it was, but she knew as adrenaline flooded her bones and turned them electric, that she couldn't let anyone see it.

Stuffing her feet into her wellies, she opened the back door. Cold air swarmed into the house, stinging the exposed flesh of her face, neck and forearms. She shut the door behind her and slogged through the quicksand-like snow towards it, stopping a few metres away.

'What are you?'

Up close, the thing had a shape that she almost recognised. Shadowy hair billowing in the wind. Ally tucked her own runaway hair behind her ear before it could blind her. The shadow mimicked her.

Her stomach churned as she regarded it. She knew this thing. Somehow, she knew it, and she wanted it gone. Now.

She lashed out with the knife in her hand, dug the blade deep into that shadowy stomach. Felt an icy sliver of pain in her own. She watched the shadow stagger back, fall down and gush black ichor onto the pure white snow. A dilution.

And then it disappeared, leaving only that lingering pain in her belly, like an echo of something forgotten. The unease in her chest settled there as if licking a wound.

'Ally?'

Danny was stood, framed by the kitchen door, holding keys in his hands. He was haloed in silver by the light and warmth behind him.

'I didn't hear you come home.' Her voice was uneven, seesawing up into the heavens. Belatedly, she realised that she was kneeling in the snow, slush beneath her shins. How long had she been here? She couldn't feel her nose.

Danny trekked through the snow to stand beside her. Slowly, he extricated the knife from between her numb fingers, and she leant towards his warmth, like a flower seeking the warmth of the sun.

He pulled her in, breathing a great sigh of relief as she allowed him. He wrapped her in his arms and took the weight off of her knees, lifting her against him.

'Come on,' he said, smiling down at her. 'Whatever you're making smells great.'

The snow had fallen in thick sheets, burying the house and its occupants in an icy tomb. Ally was in the kitchen again, flicking through a recipe book noncommittally. Nothing in its pages appealed. She wanted a strong, comforting meal, and it felt like she held the recipe to one somewhere in the recesses of her mind. A childhood memory of her grandmother's stodgy pie and thick gravy, or her mother's beef bourguignon. If she could only concentrate long enough to find it. But her mind was like cotton wool; even her memories felt distant, like she was seeing them from afar. A stranger in her own head.

An instinct long buried made her look up.

There, through the archway of kitchen to dining room, in the threshold, was the shadow. It was more corporeal now. The shadows a solid substrate that seemed to suck everything around it into a dark point. It was touching the pencil marks on the threshold, the little echoes of Ally's past heights.

And it was wearing her jumper.

The bright red one that *he* had bought for her. Tiff had bought her all-new clothes a few months ago. None of her old clothes fit her anymore.

She could call out. Scream for Tiff or Danny. She opened her mouth in exquisite agony of paralysis. If she called for them, she would be in trouble. She couldn't let them see it. Whatever this was, it was hers and it was shameful.

The shadow tilted its head as she lifted the poker from its antique rack next to the fireplace. It measured its weight, shifting to the back leg as she hefted the poker and swung it down like a baseball bat.

Pain exploded in her head, forcing her to her knees on the threadbare carpet. The poker clattered out of her hand, and she watched as, in the last convulsions of existence, the shadow reached out a hand to grasp it.

'Ally?'

Tiff skidded into the room on her sock-feet, took in the scene with a wide sweep before dropping to her knees beside Ally. She threw an arm over her back, pulling her into a crunch of a cuddle.

'It's okay,' she said, running a hand through her hair. 'You'll be okay.'

'I don't know what to make for dinner,' Ally said, barely recognising her own voice.

Tiff let out a confused laugh. 'That's alright, we'll figure it out together.'

Was there anything worse than the sound of a ringing phone? Anything more shrill and annoying? Ally rolled over in her bed and groaned. Her head felt like it was cracking open along a long-buried fault line.

Tiff and Danny mustn't be home, she thought. Bewildered, she crawled from the covers and slalomed between her dirty-clothes chair and the wall, out into the landing and towards the small table where they kept the house phone.

Reaching out a hand for it, she touched the inoffensive plastic and froze. There was something wrong. If she answered the phone, something bad would happen. Something bad was already happening. Adrenaline flooded her veins in an icy thrill. Wide eyes bounced from doorway to doorway, fighting to find the source of danger.

Nothing.

Cold fingers down her spine, a cool hand on her shoulder. Ally jerked in a circle to face the shadowy figure again.

'No!'

The sound that came out of herself was animal, and she staggered back to put space between them as it reached out a hand towards her. It was still wearing her jumper. But now it was worse; she recognised the hair spilling from its head to be her own long, blonde tresses. How *he* had loved her hair. It came to stand at the top of the stairs, following, after her retreat.

'Why are you doing this to me?'

On brittle legs, she staggered towards it, fury and fear puppeteering her arms. She grabbed the horrid shadowy face and shoved, watching as it fell down the stairs.

Pain rippled through her body, like a stone in a still river. An old friend that she remembered all too well. She slid down Danny's closed bedroom door, all the way to the floor, and watched as it disappeared once more.

How long could she keep this up? Her bones ached; her lungs burned; her skin itched. As if some giant unseen hand was turning her inside out.

The sky and the earth were smothered with snow in midwinter. Noon came around once again with Ally still in bed. She could hear the hushed mourner-like whispers of Danny and Tiff as they snuck around in their own home like ghosts. The entire house was coated in an anaesthetic silence, as if to speak louder than a whisper was to cause pain. And maybe it would.

For months now, Ally had been fighting that thing. The thing that now, after weeks of agonising and pain, had become less shadow and more human. With each death, it came back with a new piece of her.

As she watched it this time, come in through the bathroom door, it was her doppelgänger. But worse. While Ally wasted away in the bed, the thing that looked just like her was perfect. Perfectly made-up, perfect hair, perfect outfit, perfect white smile. As if Ally herself was a pale shadow of its perfection.

As it came towards her, she realised she had no energy left. No strength to stop it, no voice to call out for help, no nothing.

The doppelgänger climbed onto the bed, crawling over the mattress towards her until she hung above her like an inevitability.

'Go on then,' Ally whispered, 'do it. Hurt me.'

The doppelgänger reached out a hand and gently laid it on her cheek. 'Why?'

Her voice was soft and forlorn, like the memory of her mother kissing her on her forehead.

'Don't you want to?' Ally demanded, her heart trying to force its way out from behind her ribs, squeezing her lungs until it was hard to breathe.

'I don't want to hurt us,' she replied softly. 'I was waiting for you to stop hurting us too.'

Ally sucked in a breath that stuttered in her lungs. 'I'm scared.'

Ally smiled softly, bringing her head down and kissing her pain on the forehead. 'I know.'

On the first day of spring, Tiff and Danny sat together on the kitchen island with their heads together. Sun streamed in through the open windows. The aroma of freshly brewed coffee hung like a heavy perfume in the air.

They looked up from their conversation in unison as Ally walked in. Tiff gasped. Danny grinned.

'Hey, there she is.'

Ally fussed with the newly shorn ends of her hair, smoothed her hands down over her new curves and Tiff's choice of bright yellow sundress.

'Morning,' she said softly.

Tiff looked from Danny to Ally and then back again. She rocked in her seat as if having to burn off excess energy otherwise she would rocket away. She smiled tentatively. 'How are you doing?'

'Not good,' Ally admitted, 'but getting better. Thanks to you two.'

As if that confession had been the starter's pistol, Tiff rocketed out of her hair and half-strangled Ally in a hug. Danny came over more sedately and swept them both up.

And so passed the first day of spring.

HEARTBEAT

EMILY ROBERTSON   PINJARRA, WA, AUS

The river pulsed with life. Furious and hell-bent on destruction, snapping at the banks as it surged down to the sea. The rain had been torrential for the last week and showed no sign of letting up. From my room, I can see the water churning angrily and shudder watching it. Never again will I go near it, despite it calling to me.

I turn away from the window and focus on the assignment spread haphazardly across the old desk I've had since I was twelve. The original, white chipboard is chipping everywhere, but it's fine. Thanks to Dad, the computer is not the one from seventeen years ago.

'I just want to do something for you,' he insisted, pulling me into the local tech shop despite my protest that I did not need a new computer. He waved off my protests, arriving in the computer department.

'Your very best computer,' he announced confidently in his very dad way to the customer service person, who looked hungover and like he didn't want to be dealing with boomers.

As Dad triumphantly drove us home, I watched the bulk of the computer wobble precariously on the back seat. Who uses a desktop now?

If I'd had the energy to fight it further, I would have, but there's only so much you can fight an overzealous parent. Especially a guilt-ridden one.

So here I am having finished moving my files over from my perfectly serviceable laptop to the new fancy desktop he bought me. Back to uni and moving home at thirty—could I be anymore pathetic? Probably.

The last six months have been a mess to put it politely. Mum and Dad have grown increasingly concerned as I unravelled in no subtle way. So now after sitting in my childhood bedroom for eight weeks in a pitiful heap, I'm attempting to pick up the tatters of my ruined life and career.

'A project,' Mum chirped infuriatingly. 'That's what you need to help motivate you!'

The ever-positive Evelyn had dragged me from here to there, pushing me into craft afternoons with her friends in town. I do feel a bit bad for how I behaved, but there are only so many times a person can stand being asked 'So how come you're living at home again?' before they fly off the wall. She'd obviously been disappointed in me, but I was so far down in my own pity party that I couldn't see that I'd not only embarrassed her in front of her friends but hurt her too, until Dad had told me in his not-so-subtle way that I needed to get my act together.

'It's fine to be sad, but you can't pull everyone down with you,' he informed me before closing my bedroom door in my face, like I was fourteen again and a mouthy, hormonal beast. He was right though; I'd realised after some drinks. Not the answer, I know, but in the moment, they'd helped. So, the next morning, I'd rolled out of bed—yes, the same bed with its purple doona I'd picked out for my sixteenth-birthday room-makeover—and enrolled for my masters. Groan.

'Why did I put myself through this?' I mutter, trying to sort the mess into neatly sorted documents for my first assignment in eight years. Because you needed something to do and some way to resurrect the career you successfully burnt to the ground. Well, emotional, physical and marriage breakdowns are all good ways to accomplish that. And I'm nothing but a high achiever, so I hit the trifecta. No point dwelling on it now. The past is gone, and the future looks hazy at best.

As I slog away, the wheels slowly start turning again, rusty after so many weeks of mind-numbing nothing and so many years of no school. At the end of two hours, I confidently look around and decide I might have made a dent at least and I would need to be happy with that.

Dad is soon knocking on my door.

'Lisa, we're going out for dinner in ten minutes. Get dressed,' he says before walking away again. I groan, head in hands. A public dinner, in this town. More questions to face. More curious looks at yet another millennial to come running home, tail between their legs. I'm surprised there is no support group at this point. I'm well aware there is no point arguing, so I get dressed and make some quick effort with hair and face. Nothing crazy—it's not Melbourne after all.

We walk into the pub that hasn't changed since well before I was born. No, this is definitely not Melbourne. They might as well be opposite ends of the earth, not the country.

'Looking rather fancy there, Lisa!' called Sharon from behind the bar, her hair three different colours in a classic eighties' blowout. *Fancy?* Considering I was wearing jeans and a pretty ordinary shirt, standards must have slipped even further—was that possible? But maybe I needed to have a review of my wardrobe and really 'country' it up. Mum and Dad exchange looks as we pass the bar and head out the back to the restaurant, like I'm a ticking time bomb.

'So how did your homework go?' Mum asks overly interested,

obviously hoping to keep me engaged, to keep me from throwing a fit.

'It's not homework, Mum. It's just course work,' I reply patiently, again.

'And when are you going into campus?' she asks, arranging her napkin on her lap likes it's the ritz, not the town pub. Mum always was too classy for this place.

'I'm not,' I say, sipping the beer Dad knew I'd need to get through this. I wish he'd got something stronger.

Mum just about chokes on her wine.

'But you said you were going back!' she splutters. Lord help me.

'I'm a remote student now, Mum. I'm not tracking all the way into the city each day from here to go.' Oh wait, now that I had some of my shit together, did they think I was moving out?

'Was I supposed to be moving out into the city?' I ask, looking at them both. I'd get it if they were sick of me. After all, I'm sick of me too. Immediately they both protest so loudly the people at the next table look over.

'No, honey, we don't want you to go anywhere! You only just got home; I just didn't realise you could do it all on the line now,' she says, patting my hand.

Jesus, on the line. Might be time to buy some handrails for the bathrooms. I busy myself sculling my beer to stop myself from remarking. I can see Dad watching me. He can see the sarcastic reply on the tip of my tongue, but I'm on my best behaviour after last week's disaster at the art workshop.

While dinner is nice enough, I can see people peering from the bar down into the dining room. People I, unfortunately, know. I'm at the bottom of my third beer and looking imploringly at Dad to get me another, but he's shaking his head.

'If you want another one, you can go get it. You know where the bar is,' he says, putting the metaphorical boot down. Argh, Dad. Now if I don't, it'll just annoy me. Fine, I'm a big girl; I can do it.

'Do you want one?' I ask them both, but they're shaking their heads. Fine I'll go alone. Perhaps I'll upgrade from the beer then. I walk over to the now crowded bar. Damn it. I flag down an attendant I don't know and order two scotches. Bugger coming back up again.

'Hitting the hard stuff, hey?' asks a voice from behind me. I consider ignoring it, pretending not to hear, but it feels like a cowardly option and very un-me. Also, the hand on my shoulder is harder to ignore. As I turn

I catch an eyeful of dark, shaggy hair before being pulled into a crushing hug. I squeak, not expecting the hug or the strength of it. I'm enveloped by the distinct smell of tradesman, and as I'm released, I'm greeted by a wide smile and warm, brown eyes.

'Trent!' I reply happily, forgetting momentarily why I'm here, and am transported back by the familiar face. 'How are you?' I ask, still trying to draw further back, but he's got hold of my forearms.

'Oh, you know how it is.' He smiles, that one dimple on his right cheek flaring quickly. 'How about you? I didn't know you were home for a visit,' he asks, now releasing me to grab his drink off the bar. He nods to my own, waiting for me. I feel a bit foolish now with two, but all's well. I pay and turn to see him waiting for my answer.

'Oh, you know how it is,' I say, attempting my own carefree smile, but I can feel my fleeting happiness leaving me as reality sinks back in. He's looking around. Oh dear.

'I don't see Gavin anywhere. Did you leave him at home?' he asks, joking, drawing me away from the bar to a small table that's free near the wall. The only bonus in this never-ending tragedy is that I can see he actually doesn't know. There's nothing worse than people asking when you can see they've already been told; they just want the tale from you. Like they've missed out on the juicy bits somehow, and you'll fill them in.

'Oh, umm, he's not here,' I offer lamely. He's clearly waiting for more, so I barrel on, looking away.

'We're actually not together anymore, and I'm living at home with Mum and Dad again.' The silence from him is palpable. He's watching me, but I wish he wouldn't.

'Oh, so no more Melbourne then?' he asks, sipping his beer. I wish he'd look away from me.

'Probably not, at least not for a while. I've just started my masters.' I cringe. God, why am I offering information now? I want this conversation to end so I can go drink myself into a stupor. He smiles, gently now. Urgh, pity.

'You'll do brilliant. I always liked reading your pieces.'

'Oh, thanks.' Silence again.

'So… I should be getting back to Mum and Dad,' I offer, feeling just as lame as that sounded. He's nodding, no doubt happy to be rid of the sad case.

'Yeah, no worries, I'll see you around town then?' he asks, looking over and waving to Mum and Dad. Hell.

'Absolutely,' I reply, grabbing my excessive amount of alcohol and rushing back to the table. Mum is on me before I even get my bum back in my seat.

'Oh, so lovely to see you catching up with your friends,' she says, practically chirping again. I've no option but to down the first scotch in just about one go. The burn is welcome. Perhaps it can sear away some of the awkward I just survived.

The months pass in a now comforting routine. I thank God for high-speed internet and, funnily enough, my lovely new desktop that is a pleasure to use. I fall back into the uni routine easier than I thought was possible and am enterally grateful I don't have to travel to the city or move out. If someone had told me ten years ago I would be grateful to be living at home at thirty, I'd have had them checked in for psychiatric treatment. But here I am, if not thriving, I'm at least surviving now. They say time is a great healer, and I'd have to agree for the most part, but not everything heals; I'm reminded each time I look out the bedroom window at the surging water.

My gradually rebuilt, still shaky, confidence, has slowly solidified over the last months in my cocoon here with my parents. I feel like I've somehow stumbled upon a previous version of me, like she was tucked away in a cupboard somewhere, only just now set free.

As the anniversary of 'my life going to hell in a handbasket' approaches, I can feel my grip slipping a little on the tight reality I've wound around myself since moving home. Uni gives purpose, clarity, and a goal. Mum and Dad give unwavering support and love, something I hadn't realised was missing from my life or my marriage in Melbourne. Old friends have been trying to reconnect in the months since I came back, but as I come closer to the date, I can't let any more people in, not right now. I'm not confident I'll be able to hold it all together.

While the seventeenth of July dawns just like any other day, in my bones I know it's different. It's the secret I harbor. While I'll mention the implosion of my career if pressed, the explosion of my marriage if I must, I've not mentioned to anyone since coming home the real reason all those things happened. I head downstairs inexplicably drawn to the water, and even as I fight it, I know there is no point. I'd obviously been waiting for today, somewhere inside my broken heart I knew that.

I loved growing up in this house because of the river. Our rambling two-storey brick house rests atop a steep embankment on the east side of the river. The block is large enough that you can't see the neighbouring properties either side. I walk down the veranda steps and head off into the scrub to the left. The faintest of trails is marked here, from so many years of me taking this exact route. I have not been here in a whole year. The hill dips sharply, taking the path directly alongside the water. In the height of winter, the path can disappear completely. Today it's just damp, but the water rushes by. Winter has only just started, but the path will soon disappear.

Up ahead is the cut stump that I have used for the last twenty-five years as my chair. The old gum had been rotting, and I had asked Dad to cut it for me. He had warned me that the stump wouldn't last long, but here it still is. As if just for me. I had done my wishing, my yearning and my planning, sitting here, growing up. And as an adult, I had sat here and watched the life I had planned and built slip away faster than the water, which was now metres from me.

I brush the stump with shaking fingers before steeling myself to sit down. It's the same: damp and hard. Why I thought it would be different, I don't know. As I sit, the bush envelopes me. The smell and sounds of the trees, the damp earth, and the fresh water rushing for the ocean centre me and bring me comfort just as they always have. While I walked down, the sun had slowly began to peek its head out over the hills behind me, now beginning to light the sky and water.

As I watch the world slowly come alive again, I can hear the rustling of small animals in the bush. The buzz of insects grows louder as the air warms, and I allow myself to rest my hand on an empty abdomen for the first time in months. It was here I knew he had gone. We'd been visiting from Melbourne, had been keeping the pregnancy a secret to tell Mum and Dad in person. We'd been here only two days when the cramps came. At fifteen weeks, I had woken and known he was gone. I hadn't stayed in bed with my then husband, knowing he wouldn't comfort me but blame me. I had sought solace in my safe place. As I had sat here losing my baby boy, I had known it would be the end of the relationship we'd somehow built into a marriage.

The loss of my son brought me to my knees harder than I had expected. I blew my life and career up as grief consumed me, but my family had rescued me. Now as I watch the water, I know in my heart that he was loved beyond belief in the short time I had with him. In this beautiful place, he found his way to the next world.

I sit for hours, letting the bush come alive under the sun. As I decide it's time to go, something from the edge of my vision has me start. A huge butterfly is perched on my shoulder; how I didn't know it was there is beyond me.

'It's okay; you can go now,' I whisper to him. Gently, he leaves me, flying out over the water and downstream.

THE OUTSIDER

A FINE MATRIARCH

ANDREA McMAHON   MOONAH, TAS, AUS

Linda is the matriarch of the Medlock family. Linda is of the opinion that such a rarefied status should come with some perks. Specifically, she should be offered a roof over her head. She's not fussy. A camp stretcher in a shed out the back will do at a pinch.

Linda is seated at the bus stop after a six-hour road trip. Catching her breath. Collecting her thoughts. Donning her armour. If only she could've waltzed into town like that protagonist from *The Dressmaker*, all flaming red or bullseye black. Instead, she's had to settle for activewear, and a downmarket version of it at that. A loose T-shirt and trackpants. The undeniable reality is that Linda, once glamorous and svelte, has let herself go. It's possible she may not even be recognised by the extended family she grew up around, although she has no doubt she will recognise them. They might be older, a little fatter and greyer, but still made from the same essential ingredients: clean living, family values and wholesome home-cooked meals.

Linda, while raised on much the same diet, has over the course of the years supplemented it with a considerable quantity of her own additives. In the case of alcohol and recreational drugs, this has been—in her opinion—within generous but acceptable limits. In the case of prescription medication, however, Linda is acutely aware that she descended into addiction with frightening speed, cumulating in a stomach-pumping stint in emergency followed by some months in rehab.

She isn't about to make excuses. Yes, there had been chronic migraines, and yes, there had been doctors too lax in their prescribing of narcotic medications. But there had also been her neighbour, Marie, and the packets of oxycodone left around Marie's flat. Linda discovered them soon after she moved in next door and Marie invited her in for a neighbourly cup of tea.

It had all come out in the wash. Linda understands *quid pro quo*. Give and take. Marie's family and the police did not. The family had packed up Aunt Marie and her most treasured possessions like a bag of recycling and taken her to do the rounds of relatives while they found her accommodation in an aged care facility. Linda hopes that no matter where Marie ended up she found someone amongst the many residents and staff willing to take the time to hear about the beloved husband who died too young, the duck-egg blue house they bought when first married and in which Marie lived alone until the maintenance got too much for her. Linda knows it won't be any of Marie's relatives. They hadn't listened when she'd told them she didn't want to leave her flat.

So Linda has come back to her hometown. Where clean and drug-free family matriarchs are not left to roam the streets in search of a dry patch to spend the night. She is no prodigal daughter awaiting forgiveness. She has status in the family, and she is going to take her rightful place. She's getting ahead of herself, of course. She'll be happy to start with that camp stretcher out the back. Linda is not greedy, never has been, unless you want to count her thirst for life as greed for experience.

And experience is the one thing Linda knows she has in abundance. She's been rich, and she's been poor. She can state unequivocally that while being rich is better, being poor can be tolerable. She has gone up and up, and she has come crashing down. And she has always travelled light. When she left her up-and-coming barrister boyfriend and their Sydney apartment, she took with her two suitcases filled with designer clothing and bespoke jewellery. When she left her French husband to his IT company, slamming the door of their provincial farmhouse behind her, she took with her two cases of French haute couture, more glittering and gold accessories, and a couple of bottles of the local rosé. When she left Colin to his seafood restaurant in Byron Bay, she took with her one case of colourful beachwear, a fine collection of the local artisan jewellery, and an addiction to the prescription medication Colin had left lying around their beachside shack. Linda's migraine headaches had gotten worse. Those little pills had helped.

Linda's last separation was from her parole officer. Theirs had been a short-and-sweet liaison, and when she left, promising never to return, it was with the same backpack of T-shirts and trackpants she is now resting her feet on at the bus stop. Marie's family had wanted her charged. And yes, she had taken a few dollars now and then that she'd seen lying around the flat along with those helpful little pills. It had seemed to Linda that Marie had neither needed the money nor wanted it, and it had been easy enough to convince herself that it had been left there for her to find. *Quid pro quo*. If Marie's relatives had understood the concept they would've visited, taken their aunt to her medical appointments, delivered a few home-cooked meals, their way of giving for the generous inheritance they would be receiving upon Marie's death. Linda had made sure she'd got that out in court. It had been a small but satisfying act of vengeance.

A fine misty rain has descended upon the coast now, creating a comforting blanket around Linda, a protective layer. It had been a shock when the bus turned westward, and she'd seen once again how beautiful it was. Rolling green hills and rich red earth; the sparkling deep blue of Bass Strait. She knows she shouldn't judge her sisters for never having left this beautiful place, but she knows too that they shouldn't have judged her for wanting to leave. She took a chance for a different sort of life, and it is not a decision she will ever regret, even if she has only a backpack of activewear to show for it.

Because Linda knows that what really counts cannot be seen. It is not something that you wear like a piece of glittering jewellery, it is something that hides from the light, to be called upon when needed. Your inner strength, your resilience, that like a spring bulb will fight its way through the darkness to the light. What do her sisters know about such things? They have stayed cocooned within their comfort zones, protected by a high fence barbed with a barrage of excuses. Linda knows that Deb, with her organisational skills, could've been the CEO of a multinational corporation by now. As far as Linda is concerned, being elected president of the school parent association and secretary of the local Rotary Club doesn't cut it. And Jen, her youngest sister, might even have managed to stand on her own two feet by now if she'd given herself half a chance. She could've left that dreary husband of hers to his six o'clock news and nine o'clock bedtime. Jen might have wobbled a bit and fallen to the ground, but Linda figures that if her little sister hit the ground hard enough, she might just have discovered that she bounced.

Linda knows she is being a little hard on her sisters. They are good people. They would've brought Marie home-cooked meals, protected her from predatory next-door neighbours. But she knows too that she is the one with the net of experience that can be thrown far and wide over the family, over the children and grandchildren, as befitting a family matriarch. Sure, a net might develop a few holes over the years and need a little repairing, but it can still fling you high into the air and catch you when you come back down again. Lost and confused, battered and bruised.

Linda stands up and slings her backpack over her shoulder. It is raining heavily now. She will arrive at her sister's—which one will have the honour she is yet to decide—bedraggled as well as ragged. As she walks along the empty footpath, she notices how much the town has changed since her last visit. It has grown smaller, poorer. We've both seen better days, she thinks, as she passes a thrift shop, a takeaway, a vacant shopfront, another thrift shop. The town lacks many conveniences, but clearly thrift shops are not one of them. She stops and stares at the smartly attired mannequin in the St Vinnie's window. The mannequin is looking decidedly confident—and more than a little haughty—in a tailored crimson suit and black killer heels. Dressed like that, she could teach this dying town how to survive, she decides.

It is an outfit befitting a fine matriarch.

BLACKPOOL SOLO

DAN MICKLETHWAITE   YORKSHIRE, UK

The telecoms mast by the side of the road is a gleaming pastiche of the Tower behind. Or maybe it's just a mirage, he considers, caused by the heating and fumes on the coach. He blinks but can't shake it. Still can't believe it. He can't understand what the planners were thinking, to sully the view of their landmark like this.

Not that he's really well-placed to throw stones. His T-shirt's bright orange with a black-and-white collar—a copy of a Netherlands kit from the nineties—with a crumpled, cream golf jacket over the top. The look's rounded out by a pair of old jeans and some trainers from Lidl, their grip all but gone.

He is careful descending the steps off the coach because snapping his neck isn't quite what he's after, and neither is breaking an ankle or hip. He might not have much pride, but he does still have some. He closes his jacket to cover the shirt, and because now he's free from that motorised greenhouse, he feels the niggling coastal chill. This even though the sky's cloudless and blue, the sun like a migraine. This, and he hasn't come out with his shades.

Sighing, he squints at the wannabe Eiffel, as if the strong crosswind might rupture or warp it—something enchanting enough to dissuade him, make him revisit and alter his plans.

It doesn't.

Nor does the breeze remove, entirely, the cloying ammoniac odour of piss, from sitting too near to the toilet onboard. So pungent he hadn't dared use it himself, despite having needed to go for an hour.

He frowns at the cost of the ones in the car park, but at least hopes the fee means that they will be clean. They are, more or less, though the soap in the cubicle he picks is empty. Fortunately, he still has some anti-bac hand gel, roughly a third of a fifty-ml bottle, and he squirts it and rubs, and it stings his dry skin. A fragrance of cucumber, mellow and crisp.

The journey has left him so tired and so thirsty that he can't really focus upon what he'll do; how he'll actually end it. A small, low-key café catches his eye, a couple of streets from the cold Irish Sea.

The door chimes as he enters and disturbs the barista, who is obviously miffed to be pulled from her phone. She is maybe nineteen, early twenties at most. He barely remembers what that age was like, and yet somehow recalls being far younger still. Like Christmas, aged seven, when his family had bought him a beginner magician's set and branded him cute when he'd tried to do tricks.

Abracadabra.

'Hi, love,' she says, with a little more brightness than he'd been expecting, and his train of thought slows for some leaves on the line. He stands there and gawps like a goon for a moment before he recovers his senses and smiles. Hopefully just a polite one, not creepy.

'Can I get a black coffee, love? Please. To go.'

'Americano? You want milk with that?'

He shakes his head and then checks for the price on the wall. Roots in his jeans for the leftover coinage and cradles it all in his slightly damp palm. A shiny ten pence at the edge takes his fancy, but it might be too simple, not much of a test—he goes for a discoloured twenty instead. The Queen's face is weathered. The machine is still steaming and the barista's not watching, so he chooses to practise his old favourite skill.

Rolling it over each knuckle in turn.

Stinging or not.

He used to go by the moniker, The Magnificent Julian, at least when he dreamed about putting on shows. But it's a while since he tried, and his joints have got rusty, and it seems that he's not so magnificent now. The twenty pence slips between third and fourth fingers, clangs on the counter, and makes the lass jump.

There are parrots in Blackpool, or at the very least one. It sits on the roof of an amusement arcade, staring towards him, its oversized wing jabbing down like a threat.

Pieces of eight.

Pieces of 'ate.

The *h* remains silent, except in his head.

He stops on the pavement and eyeballs it back. It's none of your business. Leave me alone. The charred, bitter reek of the still-too-hot coffee has exiled the last of the piss from his nose. He swigs it defiantly, sticks out his blistering tongue at the bird.

Then reels it in quickly, as a blonde and her fella step out round the corner. They see him and struggle—but fail—not to laugh.

Out on the promenade, the wind has grown stronger, and while it's still not sufficient to topple the Tower, it provides a few paragliders on the beach with a lift. They're wearing what look to be powder-blue shell-suits, like a new and unusual genus of angel. Beyond them, the heavenly glare of the sea.

He blinks at the shimmer from over the road, before setting out to go watch them more closely. Almost steps into the path of a tram. He balls his free fist at his cowardice, weakness, instinctively clenching his other hand too. As the hot coffee splashes the sleeve of his jacket, he gasps and swears and fumbles the cup.

He contemplates leaving it there in the gutter, but feels like the parrot would still bloody judge him and the angels subject him to righteous disgust. So he crouches to salvage and looks for a bin.

There is one by a stall selling 'Authentic Churro's' and although there isn't much point in him eating, he quickly succumbs to their cinnamon whiff. They're properly cheap so he opts to get four. He's almost excited. But the batch that he's given is far from the finest and crumble like sandcastles caught in the tide.

He waits at the roadside, attempting to swallow, till there aren't any cars or tour buses or trams. Yet before he steps forward, a carriage rolls by—a silver-white pumpkin come straight out of Disney, except pulled by a horse that looks straight from a field. Dried mud like Rorschach blots sprayed on its flanks.

His mind jumps to Boxer from *Animal Farm*. The cartoon from the fifties, where they're building the windmill—nowt Disney in that. And then to his dad, his dad's mates, and himself, as he'd kept getting older. As his waist had expanded and his hair had thinned out and his back and his knees and his feet began aching, and the women stopped looking his way quite so often, or perhaps he had simply stopped looking at them.

The rail on the seawall is cold, a bit greasy. He clutches as if it might keep him intact. The angels are still mostly airborne and graceful, though a couple of them have now come in to land. Another is just in the process of doing so, but their wing and their blue shell-suit legs appear floppy, and it seems like they cannot control their descent. Till the very last moment, when they bend at the knees and gently alight.

Julian breathes and turns round to the Tower.

It still isn't wavering, only his bones.

His fingers have come off the railing completely, and the pastry bag too, the remnants from which are now strewn on the ground. He's inclined to retrieve them, or at least kick them over the edge to the beach, but already the seagulls have sighted and swooped. Three of them tear the last churro to shreds.

What's the collective noun for this species?

A mugging?

A shambles?

Stuff 'em, regardless. He fancies a drink.

He was thinking of beer till he got to this pub, the one by the Tower. But he's purging his hands of the germs from the railing, and the gel's hint of cucumber makes him want gin. A botanic infusion. Relics of other scents too, like a cocktail. The pastry and coffee, the coppers as well.

He stands by the window, dredging around for what's left of his change. He doubts there's enough to get anything good, and he'd come without his debit card in case he was tempted to stop and go home. There's a twenty-quid note, though he'd rather not use it. He would like to leave something apart from these clothes.

Beyond his reflection, the bright orange T-shirt, there's a lion's head made out of pale wooden slats, which takes pride of place on the wall by the stairs. Julian conjures the beast in its prime, stalking its prey on the seafront behind him. A diaphanous glimpse of its ghost in the glass. Mane made of sawdust. Haunches of pine. Snapping those gulls with its splintery fangs.

He is no longer thirsty. He takes a step back as some people emerge and veer left up a side street, towards the town's core. It is only as the last one departs that he clocks what they're holding: a diminutive coffin. An instrument case.

Intrigued, he pursues them.

A New Orleans–style funeral being what he expects.

Perhaps for the lion, or maybe himself. If a bit prematurely.

Though, none of them take out their horns yet to play.

They wend their way through streets full of cheap bed and breakfasts, some pastel but faded and others just drab. Then souvenir shops interspersed with chain restaurants, bookies and shoe shops, a handful of pubs. A couple of buskers the group don't acknowledge. A homeless man, too, with a raggedy dog.

On one road, the lampposts are curved and top-heavy and put him in mind of *The War of the Worlds*. The fifties version. He waits for a blast from a heat ray to end it, but that simply isn't the way his luck runs.

While he could try and claim that's the reason he's here, with this purpose in mind, it wouldn't exactly be justification. Most other people have bad fortune too, or at least not the best, yet he can't see them coming to Blackpool to die.

Then, he can't see them doing much of anything really, with the streets being so crowded, and because he keeps closing his eyes to the glare. Which is how he collides with the woman in front. She has come to a stop alongside her companions, who have the same emblem sewn on their shirts.

He shrinks at the thought of his own phoney outfit, but she studies him calmly, without indignation, and if there is any judgement, she's hiding it well. She doesn't seem threatened by him in the slightest—though, that might have something to do with her case. It's the biggest one there, like a battering ram, and she holds it about the same height as his knees.

'Ey up,' she says, with a broad Yorkshire accent. 'Can I help you wi' sommat? Have you got yoursen lost?'

More than you know, lass, he thinks, but can't say.

Instead, he just nods at the building behind her.

'The Winter Gardens? Not much to look at from this angle, are they? But wait till you're inside! I take it you're here for the band contest, then?'

He nods once again, supposing he will be. He still hasn't settled on method or place.

'That's great, love. This is the door for performers and judges, but if you go around to your left there'—she gestures, case swinging—'you'll find the main entrance easy enough. Hope you enjoy it!'

'Me too!' he blurts, a tad overeager, and awkwardly smiles before rushing away.

The posters in the box office tease upcoming shows, some of them weeks if not months in advance. A mixture of plays and dance troupes and comedians, a handful of whom he has seen on TV. Whether or not they're much good doesn't matter—he won't be attending.

A ticket for this contest is priced at twelve-fifty, and he's of a mind, almost, for skipping that too. But he's already at the counter, where he stands like a seagull in tram lights—if only—until he reluctantly reaches for cash.

He opens his wallet as if to do magic; it might contain flowers, or a dove, or a rabbit, or a handkerchief he can then make disappear. Yet he never quite mastered that legerdemain and has anyway noticed the stain on his coat sleeve, rusty and brown as the remnants of blood. So instead, this now feels like a tiny post-mortem, with the twenty-pound note as a kidney or lung.

There are palm trees in Blackpool. The kind parrots might nest in, though none have so far. And these are only small trees, which don't seem to bear fruit—there's no danger of coconut husks dropping down. Also, they are bedded in terracotta plant pots, rather than pristine white tropical sand, so perhaps they're not really outlandish at all.

Still, this hallway's impressive, as the bandswoman said.

He can't make out much of the pale eggshell tiling beneath all these people, but the sturdy Victorian steel of the ceiling, in polygonal arches, is painted a warm and evocative blue. The glass in between them is all slightly frosted, creating a semblance of contrails or clouds. Lanterns like inverted pyramids dangle, glowing already. It conjures a staid but remarkable glamour, an illusion that Julian's willing to buy.

So long as it's not too expensive, at least.

He fondles the coins to reduce his anxiety, the sense of being stranded in here on his own. He withdraws one at random, the shiny ten pence that he'd previously shunned. But he doesn't replace it—he needs something to help him reclaim some belief. He holds it, arm-bent, between thumb and first finger, inhaling deeply to counter the shake. Not that it matters. In spite of this hallway being crowded with people, no one is paying attention to him.

His family had likewise stopped watching his efforts when they'd judged, at age seven, he did not have the knack. His hands were too small then to shuffle cards properly, his fingers too stumpy, and he fell back too often on fifty-two pick-up, until he got left to collect them himself.

Abracadabra.

But although he had tried other hobbies thereafter, he'd continued to work on this one dexterous trick. Honed it by high school, where it gained him a first modest taste of celebrity—a much-sought distraction in history classes—before interest declined after maybe a month. If he could have persisted, expanded his repertoire, was there ever a chance he'd have topped the bill here?

Fifty-fifty. Heads or tails.

He mulls over whether to toss for it now, but the coin stays between his phalanges instead. He rolls the ten pence back and forth past his knuckles, and it crests over each like a slow ocean swell. Even glints like the tide, or the telecoms mast, yet still there is nobody paying him mind. A fair few musicians are boozing already, and Julian's thirsty and lonely, bereft.

Pieces of late.

The coin drops, rolls away on the eggshell tiled floor.

The sign by the doorway had said 'Spanish Hall', but he thinks it has more of an Italian aura, from some of the vistas he's seen on TV. He has never been out there in person, alas, and only visited the Balearic Islands once as a kid. Mallorca or Minorca. While he'd loved both the sun and the ice cream intensely, he'd never fulfilled his desire to return.

This isn't much of a substitute really, though it is still beguiling, and he can't help but stare. There's an intricate carpet around the room's edges, with a light wooden floor in the middle, beneath him, and another fine ceiling of plaster and glass. Half a dozen spectacular chandeliers, too. But those aren't the details that capture his gaze.

At a height where they could have installed some more seating, instead they'd erected a small model town. The walls have the texture of actual sandstone, or possibly churros, and the roofs contain tiny but separate tiles. Most of the trees appear sculpted as well and not simply trompe l'oeil. They stick out convincingly from the sky-painted background, and get larger, more lifelike, approaching the front, to fit with a balcony that's regular scale.

While he isn't here due to love, star-crossed or otherwise, *Romeo and Juliet* enters his mind. Not the late-nineties, gun-laden version, but a short one they'd been shown at high school for English, which he thinks had been made with stop-motion and clay. In fact, he can almost believe it was filmed here, and the play must have surely been staged in this hall.

What light through yonder window breaks?

He doesn't remember the line that comes next.

His understanding of Shakespeare has always been patchy, though it beats what he knows of brass music, hands down. Beyond a few films, he hasn't heard it in ages, at least none of this marching and coal mines malarkey, and doesn't recall being keen in the past.

The MC announces the day's first contestants, and while their name sounds familiar, and possibly Yorkshire, he isn't exactly sure where they're from. Regardless, it's clear that they must be quite famous, because cheering erupts as they stream into view.

He knows the collective noun for this species, but somehow a 'band' doesn't feel like enough. They're more of a legion. Regimental and potent. There is some kind of wonder about their conjunction and the way that their instruments, freed from the cases, seem as if they've come back from the dead.

Julian lowers his eyelids and shudders. He's been trying his best not to think about after, about ashes and dirt and how that's all there is. Now you see it, now you don't. He fumbles what's left of the change in his pocket; clenches so hard it might slip through his skin.

As they all take their seats in a horseshoe formation, he spots the woman he'd talked to, her tuba in tow. This is the lot he'd tailed from the pub.

None of them stumble, so they mustn't have got themselves too rat-arsed yet, but how good can they be if they're even just tipsy?

He should have stayed by the seafront and got drunk himself. Should have waited for all of those angels to leave and then taken his shoes off and stepped on the beach. Taken this change and the cash in his wallet and hidden them under a cairn made of shells. His license included. He should have scuffed his bare soles on the grains like a cleansing, attempted to smooth them like sea-battered glass. Should have left the towers and the parrot behind him. The Pleasure Beach, likewise, and the arcades, and the trams. Carried on walking in search of the tide. Removed his cream jacket and the counterfeit Dutch shirt; shucked off his jeans and his underwear too. Should have dropped them like bladderwrack clumps on the shoreline, and let the waves swallow his sandcastle flesh.

He doesn't know what to feel when the performance is over. His whole body shakes with the swell and the boom. The chirp of the cornets and wail of trombones. He echoes and thrums with the roar of applause. Voice of a lion.

Julian's never heard anything close. The solo especially, played on a trumpet, had messed with his chemistry, maybe for good. He might never hear anything like it again.

He cannot decide if he wants to or not. It's so long since his arteries trafficked such volume, at so high a velocity, for such a duration. It might have been only about fifteen minutes but felt more like hours or even a day. He checks the reverse of his hands for more wrinkles, a glimpse of his framework, to see if his time of departure has passed.

But he isn't a skeleton. And neither is anyone else in the crowd, in spite of their rather advanced average age. They all seem revived and excited instead, for the rest of the contest.

As Julian has never attended before, and has not bought a programme, he doesn't know what to expect from the format, let alone how the judges behind him are grading. He doubts they will call out glib comments and numbers, as if they're on *Strictly.* He is uncertain whether to stay and find out.

He could perhaps stand to face more of this music. To catch-up, belatedly, with this overlooked genre—how many brass bangers has he missed through the years? He half-rises then sits again, a handful of times, then remains in his chair as the next legion enters.

He squeezes the coins in his trembling fist. He is hungry and parched. He is hot and perspiring, and unzips his coat. He closes his eyes, getting braced for new marvels.

Until they start up with the same bloody tune.

There are palm trees in Blackpool and a pirate ship too. But still no more parrots, and he's grateful for that. And no outsize felines, of timber or fur.

He starts to relax, as he stands in this room that is styled like a galleon; more Spanish to him than the titular hall. It has portholes and skylights and pocked, ornate crossbeams, and the wood appears warm in the chandeliers' glow. There's an easing of pressure inside of his skull, and he feels like he should get a drink while he's here.

Though, what's left of his money might not be enough. Unlikely to stretch to a cocktail, some gin. And he can't make his legs walk across to the bar, which is already heaving. There are a few places he could attempt queuing, but bandspeople mill with their shirts and insignia, and he doesn't quite feel as if he can intrude. They all have their cases, which he does not want to knock. The instruments trapped in their coffins again.

The image makes Julian flinch, heavy breathing.

He lurks like a stowaway, hunched, unassuming, until something barges the back of his knees. He nearly falls forwards, and stumbles around to confront his attacker, but the broad, bearded face carries no sign of threat. In fact, it even seems vaguely familiar, though Julian can't put his finger on why.

'Sorry,' the man says. 'I can sightread with the best of 'em, but I can't chuffin' see where I'm swinging my gear. You're about my fifth victim, and I doubt you'll be the last.' He lifts up the case—not as large as the tuba—and offers a firm but conciliatory hand. Julian takes it, albeit slowly, still trying to think if he knows him and how.

'I'm Geoff, by the way. Let me get you a beer.'

Julian's silent.

'Unless it's too early? Don't fret, we won't judge. What happens in Blackpool stays in Blackpool. You know, like Las Vegas, but wi' more fish and chips.' He grins and pats Julian hard on the shoulder. 'Cool shirt, an' all. They had a great bloody line-up. Bergkamp and Overmars. Both the de Boers. I still can't believe they never won a World Cup.'

'I know, right?' says Julian. 'And Kluivert as well.'

'Aye, an' Edgar Davids, with them glasses like Bono!'

Julian laughs, and the pressure's eased further, and he finds that his legs have remembered to walk. He has twigged why the man's recognisable, too—he had played the first solo, brought the whole audience under his spell.

Abracadabra.

They are served straightaway upon reaching the bar: two pints of bitter, surprisingly cheap. The bartender waits as Geoff delves in his pocket, and Julian watches the trumpeter's hand. It is small, almost childlike, and the fingers seem stumpy. But when they unfurl, there are pounds, fifties, twenties, and a ten pence that shines like the cold Irish Sea.

CARAVAN THERAPY

SHOSHANNA ROCKMAN   ELSTERNWICK, VIC, AUS

Afterwards, I could barely bear to look at photos.
My eyes stung, as though from onions, chlorine
(without goggles), and eyelashes
growing in reverse.

But after Covid, I took that timely (overdue) trip
and landed in the field, where *it* squatted silent,
stolid and profound. I peered
from around corners

until my gaze buckled — it flattened and unkinked.
Until I could stare without blinking (or thinking)
too much. Until I approached
to eyeball its dark

windows, then darted away to the (cover of) trees.
One day I peeked inside its gloom. My entrails
made themselves known, knowing
what I knew I wanted

to forget. And to remember. Then the rains. Winter
drizzled. I stayed dry, away and wary. After a lull,
I rallied, pressed my nose against
the (grimy) glass,

even tried the levered handle. The dwarfish door gave
it all away. I stood inside the space which shrank
away from me and stirred
(a little) less of me,

so that the next intrusion saw me barge straight in.
I opened every cramped cupboard, pulled out
every drawer and found (almost)
nothing that had been his.

I swivelled. I saw. Surf stickers stuck to the side wall.
Peeled each one off in turn. (Privately) pocketed.
I skipped down the three front steps. The last
dangled like a milk tooth.

SOMEBODY

SUE PINCHAM   EAST CORRIMAL, NSW, AUS

He swaggered down the main street with his dogs, past the empty shops and the occasional greasy spoon, his hair long and flowing at the back, the bald spot on top no bother to him when his dogs were by his side. They were tiny things, a fluffy, white one, and a rust-and-white terrier of some sort. He had trained them well; they didn't need a leash. Sometimes they walked a few steps ahead of him, but they always stayed close.

He swaggered past the tattoo parlour where the girls sat outside wearing black, some stoned on something, the others chatting. He knew some of them, and they nodded. This was their space. He walked on, and a child ran up to him to look at the dogs and pat them. He smiled. He was somebody. These dogs made him somebody.

An indigenous man grabbed his hand; he clasped it, said a couple of words and kept moving. The dogs gave him momentum. Movement, purpose, direction.

His dogs loved him, even a stranger could see that. Every now and then, the little white one would look back and wag its tail and wait for him.

A blonde woman, a junkie, walked beside him for a while; she had a dog like the terrier. Buster she called him, she said. Yeah, he said. He walked too fast for her; she couldn't keep up.

He kept on walking, in time with his dogs, not missing a beat.

LIFTING THE PALL

MATTHEW PITT   FORT WORTH, TEXAS, US

The dress shirt buttons no longer clasped along his client's chest.

Additionally, the man's pant cuffs rode to his calves, as if to avoid standing water. An, all in all, minor issue. Bloating, three days after a body's expiration—even this amount—was typical. Hardly worth bothering the bereaved about.

"I'll get your mortal coil in shape," pledged the undertaker, chuckling as he checked the time. At dawn, he'd summon the tailor to let out pinched, puckered places. Done well, this suit could yet survive the service. Families wanted their dearly departed decked out when ferried to the afterlife, a desire he took seriously. Even in cases like today's. This client's adult children consented only to speak over conference call, enervated not by grief, it seemed, but the conversation itself. He'd nudged the children to describe textures of their father's life: his triumphs, his passions. Doing so often put wind back in the survivors' sails. From these two, he'd been unable to wrest a single anecdote.

These were tomorrow's concerns. Now, he was expected at a party. He eyed his client makeup table, batted rouge on his face, and locked up.

"You're only barely early!" the party hosts yelled in mock exasperation when he arrived. "Did you have to work late? Surely *your* customers can't be that demanding."

The undertaker almost blurted the macabre standard joke of his profession—"Now, you *know* undertakers must keep a tight lid on our business."—but for some reason, stopped himself, mumbling jovially instead about getting distracted on his way over.

His behavior followed its normal patter: downing two plates of food (one at the party's onset, another during a lull), meeting three strangers, slugging four drinks, including a brisk coffee to slough off his booze buzz. But with each hour and conversation, the undertaker's mood darkened.

He became alert to, and concerned by, his part in the amusements. Hosts always asked that he arrive early. Eager to see him? Or because it permitted others to show fashionably late? Witty women beckoned him into groups, relaying jokes and gossip, as he laughed and swayed at their sides. Snaring his wrist when he eyed a drink refill, imploring, *Don't leave me!* He'd return home satisfied, lofty perfume traced on his sleeves, filled with canapés and cognac he never felt at ease storing in his drab apartment. Tonight, he saw these moments differently: a straight man needed to hold crowd interest, attract onlookers. A background player blending with the boisterous, no more than a wall for bigger-than-life voices to bounce off. It left him cross and sleepless. When he tried sinking into his pillow, party memories merged with that earlier awkward chat with his client's children. "Dad liked baking cakes!"; "Always punctual!"; "That's right! Back from work by 5:40, dinner on the table by half past six." Each detail of their father a struggle to conjure. Facts to discard. His client's obituary would be so scanty and skeletal! Everything in it reflecting how he'd aided his children's lives, not a scrap about his own. Even arranging a time to meet these children tomorrow had proven arduous. As if an inconvenience. Ingrates! thought the undertaker, unsure if he meant the kin, the party guests, or both.

On his morning return to the mortuary, a disturbing sight greeted the undertaker.

His corpse client had revolted against the casket's cushioned confines overnight, as if a bread loaf spilt from a baking tin due to excess yeast. Fattening feet split open shoes. Hair tufts poked out of the casket top like wild bristles from a painter's brush.

Though no longer viable, this body was not at rest. Grown in his absence. Growing still.

The casket groaned. The undertaker recoiled. The lid when he tried to shut it would not quite clamp, his client's face inching it upward, like attention-starved actors peeking after a stage curtain's closure. The face's pallor had not gone green, as it will once the organs cease work.

No fabric alterations could possibly conceal this rupturing.

No sooner had he canceled with the tailor than the client's children rang his front bell.

They would expect to see their father in an artfully arranged state of peace. Not pretzeled in a box like a furtive stowaway. He hoisted the body. He could move it into a larger casket, similar style, at his own expense. But how long would that new shelter contain the client? Would his corporeal form continue like some hermit crab to broaden and lengthen? Up until his funeral, or further?

The relatives rang again.

This visit was fraught in the best circumstances. Even if these children were ingrates, this was a time for condolence, not fresh shock. Only pall should grow in such a moment. Brushing rouge on his perspiring forehead, the undertaker shut the antechamber, burying this secret while he constructed a coherent plan.

He welcomed the progeny with stalling pleasantries, touring them by parlors incidental to their purpose, relaying history they hardly needed to hear, constructing rococo questions to distract from the pressing matter. For a time his tactics worked: as before, the pair seemed tranquil, content to go where told. They trudged two steps behind, breaths smelling of charred toast. A faint decay not present in the parent who should have been emitting such an odor; should have been losing hold and composition, but instead, vexingly, had expanded in the vein of some minor universe. Just one room from where the living sat to consult.

The undertaker indicated chairs, with cushioned taupe backs shaped like violins. "I am—truly sorry for your sorrow."

The progeny sighed, disbursing charred-toast exhalations, disappointed, perhaps, to hear one who trucked in mortality lean on trite phrases. The undertaker continued cycling through shopworn sentiments (*cut down in his prime, best days ahead*), nervously noting the casket creaking one room over. Creaks growing louder. As if they sat on a ship's prow, rocking gently at sea.

He recalled, years ago, a competitor's woes—yes, funeral homes competed for the dead—over an issue with a cemetery's water table. Some tendency in the soil to soften into loamy cakes which crack, thus pushing coffins upward, inch by profane inch, until they beached upon blades of grass. At first the funeral home dug deeper than the standard six, satisfied this plunge would keep coffins submerged. But they bubbled up again, breaking through the tomb's sacred consecrated soil, like some perverse, incomplete resurrection. His rival never recovered from this blow to reputation.

How long could the undertaker elude *this* strange turn?

"I need to brace you both," he said, "for a sight I can scarcely conceive of myself."

He issued his awkward report. Assuring them he'd followed painstaking protocol with their father, bathing and disinfecting his body in keeping with medical arts. Staging the dearly departed for brief preservation and presentation. Preparing to swap blood for embalming fluid. Yet all was not going to plan. This body had a mind of its own. What the undertaker mistook for bloat was in fact physical progression. At a time when autolysis should take hold, the flesh absorb itself, this stricken man was, well, expanding. The undertaker snuffed a scented candle on a table by his knees. Fingers gliding on its hardening slick, whorls from his tips digging gently into paraffin like his boyhood skate blades over lake ice. Happier times. He bent to the candle with each revelation of hard truths. In imitation, he supposed, of bowing. Well, he would bow low as they needed. He was beyond bowing. He was near to begging.

At last he turned around.

Torqued faces greeted him—not in the sad moues or ruddy rage he expected. "He is growing?"

"Growing," the sister repeated, her voice harboring not disgust but vagrant joy.

"Please understand," the undertaker labored to clarify, "there is no breath." He was more mortified than ever. He'd led them astray, stirred clouds of magical thinking, made them imagine their loved one was somehow restored, respirating, good as new! "No brainwave activity. Your father is gone. Only cellular growth continues rampantly..."

The progeny clutched hands. Astonished. "We understand! He's a medical marvel?"

"Well... yes. Though a marvel, I stress, presenting no perceivable benefit."

"Not for him," the son agreed. "Or us. But one who would warrant interest from researchers? And surely, scientific journals?"

The daughter patted the undertaker's palm, noting *his* agitation. "Yesterday you asked us to relay the kind of man Father was? When we dodged you, we weren't trying to be unhelpful. It wasn't from fear of opening floodgates. What's dented us most is how Father never let us *see* who he was. All we knew for certain was... he was uniformly small."

"Slight. Timid in public, through and through."

"King of echoes," the daughter concluded. "Though he hardly set out to be. And went to his grave certain he'd duped us."

Awaiting more, the undertaker patted his lapel pocket square, ensuring it rested at the ready to dab and, by its cloth, console. But the son asked only if the undertaker could relight the candle cooling on the low table. "I found its scent and flicker... uplifting."

"And once it burns for a bit," the daughter added, "may we view him?"

The candle shone again; the children's stories gathered in flocks. As though its flickering wick were a recording device indicator. They explained fantastical fabrications, told by their father from the first time their ears knew to absorb story. Described his habit of inserting himself in any significant newspaper article absorbed with morning prune juice, as his kids rose. A trade agreement brokered? He'd served as chief negotiator. A school ringing not with bells but with gunfire? He'd disarmed the shooter. Infiltrated a terrorist compound in one continent. Completed, in another, a double-blind study of new Parkinson's medication. Accomplishing each majestic task between the time the yellow bus arrived each morning and the time he began cooking dinner.

Not an ounce of it true. But it mesmerized the children, had them anticipating breakfasts with bated breath, eager to hear his latest expedition. For years it held the both of them at bay.

"At bay from what?" asked the undertaker.

"Our mother. She was erased early from our lives in a horrific sudden yank. So much so, we couldn't see her to say goodbye. For months we didn't sleep, telling ourselves it wasn't death at all, only a vanishing. And it was. But one Father had to face head-on. It must've been so hard. To look at her loss without flinching, then have to design some way forward for the rest of us..."

"He took a new job; sturdy but hated. Buried his aspirations for short hours and security. But he knew how much we were hurting. Saw the rut we were in. Needed to remove us from it."

"Learning your father had actually averted a train wreck while we were learning times tables?" the daughter asked. "That makes any serving of oatmeal enjoyable."

"But he couldn't stop fueling his legend. Even when we were ready for normal. For oatmeal." As we grew in inches and pounds, our suspicions swelled too. We unearthed a litter of continuity and timeline errors. His claims about Tuesday could not be true, if what he'd done the day before was real, too. And why did newspapers never mention him by name when reporting exploits? "So we followed him on morning ferry commutes."

"It was stranger than we imagined. Every day, his birthday."

"I'm not sure I—?"

"He'd tell fellow ferry riders it was his birthday," said the son, "so they'd be obliged to chat, keep company. He'd work different decks each week, adjusting departure times, exploring aft one morning, stern the next."

"Same thing at work. A typical day involved him calling Taipei or Rio to detail soft earnings projections, slowed production, irate consumers— the bearer of all bad news. Calls that began politely and ended with rancor. He was a small enough company cog to move without notice from floor to floor. So he soothed his nerves by setting up shop in some breakroom, wearing festive hats, lighting candles until a crowd of curious onlookers strolled in and sung to him. Strangers honoring and celebrating him, no matter how rough that week had gone."

"His one pleasure. Enjoying nibbles of cakes he'd baked and inscribed his own name upon."

"As adults, it grew harder to keep connected. We couldn't work up the courage to confront Dad over his lies. He, in turn, kept feeding them. Did he need us to keep seeing him as grand? Or was it what he needed for himself?"

"Either way—at last, he has his legacy."

Hearing this fraudulent fixation moved the undertaker. Had he not done the same, believing himself to be the life, and not the background, of parties? And the same in service to the snuffed lives of others? Etching legacies of his clients' beloved? Hoping mourners would be moved by his efforts to elevate the lost, that regaling their litanies of deeds and talents at funerals would add lustre to his dingy own? He returned to the paraffin. Scored marks smoothed over. He used to skate the lake as a boy feverishly, joyfully, but doing so only after dusk—so no eyes would witness when he flopped, when he failed. When had he taken to keeping his pursuits and passions invisible to others?

"Let me bring you to see him," the undertaker suggested. "I warn you, he will appear out of proportion."

The son rose confidently. "That's what excites us."

The chamber's coolness seemed to lend the children courage to approach. By this point, the casket lid was propped significantly by the expansion of its resident, making lifting it an easy matter. The daughter admired the split stitches of her father's suit. Thrilled at swollen fingers she couldn't form a fist around. With pride, the son announced: "Look at him. Enormous. Uncontainable. You wouldn't dare commit a crime in his presence. Or break a brokered peace treaty."

"Larger in death than in breath," marveled the daughter, straightening his tie over the exposed and unbuttoned chest flesh. "If he had to leave us, what better way?"

The two happily considered unexpected expenses ahead. New suit, new casket. Perhaps an enlarging of the family plot? Plus all the time needed to sound the clarion call. Targeted invitations so professionals might circle the casket in profound disbelief, to take measure of this man. Then raise a circus tent to host a parade of media and onlookers. A party of gobsmacked goodbyes. It had taken this man his whole life—had *taken* his life—to reach a perch where people would line up to pay respects and wonder. His children would pay that same debt, thankful for the mornings he unmoored them from grief with his first, fanciful tales of possibility.

So they celebrated: both this failed man, and the glowing glory exuding from his fallen form.

THE LAST TEN SECONDS

GRACE KELLER   DALLAS, TEXAS, US

CHARACTERS

Lila Evergreen—snarky, defensive, conflicted and confused. Low self-worth hidden by "tough" exterior

Jimmy—has a similar vibe to a tour guide. 100% genuine in everything he says

Lulu (little Lila)—very sweet, very talkative. Hyperactive, almost

L.E. (teenage Lila)—angry at everyone, but mostly herself

Old Lila—most similar in personality to Lulu. She's happy with how her life turned out and, most importantly, she's forgiven herself and is finally at peace

SET

A plain wooden chair set in the middle of the stage.

THE LAST TEN SECONDS

[*Lights up on Lila standing next to the wooden chair. She looks puzzled. She's startled by a pleasant voice as Jimmy comes onstage.*]

Jimmy: Lila! So nice to see you. Why don't you take a seat?

Lila [*remaining standing*]: Who are you?

Jimmy: I'm your guide!

Lila: Guide to what? Where are we?

Jimmy: That is an excellent question, Lila. Do you know what purgatory is?

Lila: Not really.

Jimmy: It's nothing bad! We aren't exactly in purgatory, per say, but we're in its nicer, safer cousin.

Lila: Does this nicer, safer cousin space have a name?

Jimmy: Let's call it the Waiting Room.

Lila: There's no way this is real. I'm dreaming, aren't I?

Jimmy: A dream! A fun idea, but no.

Lila: So, you're saying that I've somehow been kidnapped by a college tour guide? Yeah right. Stop being so vague and just tell me what's going on. You know what? Don't even bother. I'm very independent, so I'll find my way out by myself.

Jimmy: While it would be fun to watch you try, I'm afraid your efforts would be futile. You are the only exit.

[*Lila stops pacing and stares at him like he's an idiot.*]

Lila: What?

Jimmy: Sorry, are you deaf? I know how to sign—

Lila: Shut up or I'm going to throw something at you.

[*She looks around for something to throw, then in frustration kicks the chair. Jimmy calmly watches from his original position.*]

Lila, resuming: You don't get to kidnap me, bring me to this dusty… room? Is that what you'd call it? And then put on this false "happy" face and expect me to comply? What is this, good cop bad cop?

Jimmy: I'm not a cop—

Lila: SHUT UP! You are going to answer all my questions, or I'm going to throat-punch you, do you understand? [*Jimmy doesn't reply, just looks down at her.*] Answer me!

Jimmy [*saluting*]: Yes ma'am.

Lila [*letting out a frustrating sigh*]: Fine, whatever. First question: who ARE you?

Jimmy [*cheerful*]: Jimmy!

Lila: NO! I meant what's your real name? Who do you work for?

Jimmy: The first question is easy to answer. My real name is Jimmy. I picked it out myself. The second one… well, that's more complicated.

Lila: Start talking.

Jimmy: It's kind of a long story.

Lila: I'm a black belt. Start. Talking.

Jimmy: Alright, alright. Suit yourself, black belt. I don't really work for anyone. I'm part of a larger system, yes, but I work pretty much alone. I'm a Post-Mortem Pre-Celestial Soul Welcomer and Transition Specialist, in the subdivision of Premature Afterlife Counseling.

Lila: What?

Jimmy: Think of me as your specially assigned afterlife lawyer/therapist.

Lila: What is an afterlife law—am I dead??

Jimmy: Oh shoot, did I forget to mention that?

Lila: YES!

Jimmy: Sorry, sorry. I get so excited to meet my people—

Lila [*realization hitting*]: Oh god. Oh god.

Jimmy: Like I said, you might want to sit down. Whoa! [*He catches Lila, who's gone weak in the knees, and guides her to the chair.*] Once you catch your breath, I'm assuming that you'll have more questions for me. Please, take your time.

Lila: Man, when you said this was purgatory, I didn't think you meant, like, Purgatory purgatory.

Jimmy: Well, like I said, that's not really a good name. We are in what is essentially a waiting room.

Lila: And what are we waiting for? Peter and his judgment at the Pearly Gates?

Jimmy: Nope, your death.

Lila: What?

Jimmy: Seriously, are you deaf? I really can sign if that would make you more comfortable. [*Lila glares daggers at him.*] Okay, okay, I'll stop offering. Just part of the procedure.

Lila: I'd kill you if you weren't already dead.

Jimmy: I'm not dead, thank you very much! I actually can't die. Part of the whole "immortal being" gig.

Lila: Wh— okay. Doesn't matter. Moving on. Did you say we were waiting on my death?

Jimmy: Oh, so you did hear me! That's great. Yes, we're waiting on your death, which will happen in approximately ten seconds.

Lila: WHAT? You tell me this now? Oh god. I have no time. What about my family? My apartment? I have a dentist appointment next Wednesday that I've already rescheduled. They are not going to be happy with me. Oh no, my time's up. I can feel it. Ahhhhhh!

[*Lila curls in a ball and falls to the floor, wailing in fear. Jimmy stands quietly next to her. When the wailing stops, Jimmy reaches down and pats her shoulder.*]

Jimmy: Did you get it all out?

Lila [*muffled, still curled in a ball*]: I hate you.

Jimmy: Why?? I thought I'd been perfectly polite.

Lila [*raising her head*]: You tricked me! You said I only had ten seconds left.

Jimmy: And I told the truth. I don't have the capacity for lying.

Lila: Then how am I still here?

Jimmy: We are trapped in an interdimensional pocket, outside time and space. In your physical body, the one lying on the street outside your apartment, you only have ten seconds left. Here, however, we have as much time as you want, and when we are done here, those ten seconds will be up.

Lila: Like in *The Lion, the Witch and the Wardrobe.*

Jimmy: Precisely! We are in the Wardrobe. Wow, that is a way better name than the Waiting Room. I'm gonna have to write that one down.

Lila: Jimmy.

Jimmy: Yes, Lila?

Lila: Why am I here?

Jimmy: Because you're about to die!

Lila: Please don't sound so happy when you say that.

Jimmy: Sorry.

Lila: I meant why am I here in a… wardrobe… instead of just going to Heaven or Hell or whatever else there is? Why was I pulled out of my body early?

Jimmy: See, most people just live or die. It's that simple. Enough good or bad to be sorted right away into their personal afterlife. But you, my friend, were surrounded by too much gray to be placed in that black-and-white system.

Lila: You speak in riddles and it makes me angry.

Jimmy: Go me! Anyways, that's where Lulu comes in! [*calling offstage*] Lulu! Come on in.

[*Lulu enters, carrying in her arms a large doll.*]

Jimmy: Lila, this is Lulu. She's—

Lila: She looks just like me when I was a kid.

Jimmy: Good job! She IS you as a kid, and so she's the first part of our process to getting you out of here.

[*Lila looks confused.*]

Jimmy: Okay, let me try to explain it better. Um... oh! You know that phrase that people use where they say their "life flashed before their eyes"?

Lila: Yeah...

Jimmy: Well, when you die, your life doesn't really "flash" before your eyes. Actually—

Lulu [*confidently*]: Basically, you're going to talk to little you, teenage you, and grownup you. This'll give you a look at your life. Is that good?

Lila: Yeah, that's good. I'm assuming you're Little Me?

Lulu: The Littlest.

Jimmy: Hey! Wait! I need you to answer a question first. Do you want to die?

Lila: What?

Jimmy: If you want to die, then you don't need to do all this. We can just move you on to the next part of getting into the afterlife and skip all the hassle. Sometimes the system gets messed up and puts a black-and-white person into a gray person box.

Lila: Wh— How am I supposed to know if I'm ready to die? What does that even mean?

Jimmy: I'll take that as a no, then. Alright, Lulu, proceed!

Lulu: Hi! I'm Lulu.

Lila [*looking from Jimmy to Lila*]: Wh—

Lulu [*leaning in confidentially*]: Don't worry about what he says. Half the time he doesn't know what's going on.

Jimmy: Well, that's not very nice—

Lila [*very done with Jimmy*]: Wonderful. What are we supposed to talk about?

Lulu: You. Hey! Wanna see my doll?

Lila: Uhhh, sure...

[*Lulu holds up the doll she has in her arms. It's very detailed.*]

Lulu: Look at her eyes! They have real lashes. Isn't that crazy? And every morning I do her hair up in bows and dress her and everything!

Lila: She's very pretty. Where'd you get her?

Lulu: Daddy gave her to me for my fifth birthday, remember?

Lila: Yes, I remember now! This was my favorite doll. I used to sit and play with her for hours—I'd have lots of tea parties and concerts and—

Lulu: And walks! Yeah, that's what I do with her. [*Suddenly switching topics*] How old are you?

Lila: I just turned twenty-six.

Lulu: Ooh, you're old.

Jimmy: Lulu—

Lulu: Haha, just kidding! [*She was not kidding.*] How's life going?

Lila: Alright, I guess. Or it was, before I died. [*Turning to Jimmy.*] How did I die, anyways?

Jimmy: Well, you haven't technically died yet, but you were hit by a car in front of your apartment. You were so focused on other things that you didn't see a car that was turning onto the street and stepped right in front of it.

Lila: Ugh, what a terribly cliché way to die.

[*Jimmy shrugs.*]

Lulu: Hey! Back to me! [*Lila turns to her.*] So! Is adult life everything we thought it would be? Do you have any pets? A husband or wife? Do you live in the big city and party every night and make lots of money?

Lila: Yes to big city, no to pets, no to spouse, no to parties every night, no to lots of money...

Lulu: Sounds like an awful lot of "no's" to me.

Lila: Yeah, I guess it does.

Lulu: Well, you said you were happy, so I guess that's all that matters. How's our family?

Lila: Jonah and Will are great, and—

Lulu: Who are Jonah and Will?

Lila: They're our little brothers. Mom has them when we're nine.

Lula: How are Mom and Dad? Have they stopped fighting?

Lila: Well—

Jimmy: Sorry, ladies, but that's all the time we have for today.

Lulu: But we just started talking! Five more minutes? Please, please, please.

Jimmy: One more question, and that's it.

Lulu: No fair!

Jimmy: Fine, two.

Lulu: Fine. [*She turns back to Lila.*] Do you still write and paint and take walks and play outside? Do you still give concerts and tea parties all the time?

Lila: Not really.

Lulu: Why not?

Lila: I—I don't know. Life got busy, I guess.

Lulu: Aw, that's sad. Your life doesn't sound very fun.

Lila: No, it is!

[*Lulu is unconvinced, and though she tries not to show it, so is Lila.*]

Jimmy: Alright Lulu, time to go.

Lulu [*sadly*]: Okay.

[*Lulu takes Jimmy's hand and starts walking offstage, but at the last second breaks away and runs back to give Lila a hug.*]

Lulu: Remember to have fun sometimes, pretty please.

[*She hands Lila her doll, then runs back to Jimmy, who walks her offstage. Lila sits and looks at the doll thoughtfully until Jimmy comes back.*]

Jimmy: That was so fun! How're you feeling?

Lila [*defensive, hugging the doll*]: Fine. Great. Why wouldn't I be?

Jimmy: No reason, no reason. I was just checking. Don't suffocate your doll. [*Lila loosens her grip, embarrassed.*]

Lila: It's just—

Jimmy: It's just what?

Lila: I was such a happy kid. Did you see how confident I was? How honest and outspoken and—

Jimmy: And carefree? Yes, I did.

Lila [*half to herself*]: I wish I was still like that.

Jimmy: Why aren't you?

Lila [*quietly*]: I don't know.

[*There's a slight pause. Lila shakes her head, clearing it.*]

Lila: Whatever, it doesn't matter. What's next?

Jimmy: Are you sure that—

Lila: What's. Next.

Jimmy: Okay! The next version of yourself is roughly ten years older. She turned sixteen last month. Unfortunately, she is running late…

Lila: Sixteen?

Jimmy: Yes. Is that a problem?

Lila: No, just—nevermind.

Jimmy: Okay, if you say so. Oh! Before she comes in, I need to ask you again. All part of the process. Do you want to die?

Lila: What kind of a question is that?

Jimmy: A simple yes or no question.

Lila: Oh, duh! Sorry, I forgot that I was an idiot.

Jimmy: No need to be so sarcastic. I am a very literal being; I answer very literally.

Lila: Yeah, well, how would you feel if you were constantly being questioned about whether or not you want to live? It's never been more than a hypothetical before, and now I'm supposed to know? I'm twenty-six! I've never thought about this stuff before!

L.E: Am I interrupting something?

[*Lila and Jimmy look up see L.E. standing by the place where Lulu went offstage, crossing her arms over her chest and a scowl on her face. She clearly does not want to be here.*]

Jimmy: Ah, you're finally here! Lila, meet your sixteen-year-old self, L.E.

Lila: Wow.

Jimmy: What?

Lila: My goth phase did not suit me.

L.E.: Yeah, being an adult makes you look ugly too, so don't think you're better than me.

Jimmy: Whoa whoa whoa, can we be civil please?

Lila: I'm literally just talking to myself, it doesn't matter. [*Jimmy gives her a look.*] Fine. What are you here to ask me?

L.E.: I don't know.

Lila: You don't KNOW?

L.E.: No.

Lila: Isn't your whole job here to ask me questions? Learn about the grown-up world and your future and everything?

L.E.: After seeing you here and seeing the way you died, I know enough to realize that the future isn't any better than the present.

Lila: What is that supposed to mean?

L.E. Well, let me refresh your memory. Mom and Dad are on the brink of a divorce. Their fighting? Constant. Almost as constant as my bad grades. I just found out that I didn't get cast in the school musical. And! My boyfriend dumped me on the eve of my sixteenth birthday. So, excuse me if I'm not thrilled to see that my future is lonely, angry, absent of style AND ON TOP OF ALL OF THAT cut short.

[*There's silence after she finishes. She's breathing heavily and looking at the ground. Lila looks at her, slightly shocked.*]

Lila: I'm so sorry—

L.E.: Yeah, because saying sorry is going to fix the fact that I'm a loser forever.

Lila: But you're not! You go to college and meet new people and get a dog. We live in an apartment and have a good job—

L.E.: If life is so good, then why are you here?

Lila: What do you mean? I died. It's not like I had a choice.

L.E.: Is that what he told you? [*She turns to Jimmy.*] Man, I knew you were bad at explaining things, but I didn't think you just left things out. What kind of a guide are you?

Lila: Hold up. [*She turns to Jimmy.*] What is she talking about?

Jimmy: I told you about the gray and the black and the white—

L.E.: Forget the color nonsense! Here's what happened. You got hit by the car, yes? Well, fun fact: It wasn't enough to kill you.

Lila: What? So then how am I here?

L.E.: Because you weren't strong enough to fully live, either. You would have had to work to stay alive while the paramedics rushed you to the hospital. But you didn't. You just didn't have the will to wake up. You, even as you could feel your soul trying to escape your body, couldn't figure out whether it was worth it to go back to your life. That's why Lulu and I had to come talk to you. Looking at us will hopefully make your indecisiveness go away. OBVIOUSLY that hasn't happened yet, because you're still here! I hate you even more than I hate myself.

[*There is silence, again. Lila is looking in horror from Jimmy to L.E. and back again. She wobbles and Jimmy reaches out to catch her.*]

Lila: Don't touch me!

Jimmy: I'm sorry I didn't explain it in more detail. I was trying to be delicate.

Lila: Delicate? About my subconscious death wish? So THIS is why you kept asking me if I wanted to die. Because you didn't think I wanted to live! If you're an angel, you're the worst one out there.

Jimmy: I'm truly sorry, Lila. I don't know what to say.

L.E.: There isn't anything you can say, man. She's dead at twenty-six, with no purpose and no point to life.

Lila: Shut up.

L.E.: What? I'm just telling the truth.

Lila: No, you're not.

L.E.: What?

Lila: I know that life is really hard for you right now. It seems like there's nothing good coming. But you can't just turn your back on the world. That's such a dumb thing to do.

L.E.: Isn't that exactly what you did?

Jimmy: I'm so sorry to interrupt, but we're way over our time limit. L.E., you have to leave.

L.E. [*with a dry laugh*]: It's kind of funny, right? First everyone else leaves—family, friends, lovers—and now even I'm leaving you. Not even you can stand to live with yourself. Good luck with the whole death thing. Hopefully you figure it out pretty soon.

[*L.E. walks offstage without looking back. Lila watches her leave, while Jimmy watches Lila.*]

Lila: Was I really like that?

Jimmy: I'm afraid so.

Lila: I don't know how anyone could stand to be around me. I was so mean. [*She realizes and turns to Jimmy.*] I'm sorry. I had no right to blow up at you. You're only trying to do your job, and I've been making it difficult every step of the way.

Jimmy: You didn't know. Meeting your young self is difficult—it's like holding up the harshest mirror to yourself. You see all your flaws in bright daylight.

Lila: I needed it. Oh, wow. I am awful.

Jimmy: Don't be too hard on yourself.

Lila: How can I not be? For the past ten years I've been playing the victim. TEN YEARS. I complain about my parents, my job, my boyfriend. Do you want to know what happened a month after my sixteenth birthday?

Jimmy: Sure.

Lila: My ex, Mark, called. He told me that the reason he had broken up with me was because he had been told that night that he was moving to another state, and he was so panicked about it that he had immediately called me and ended things. He was scared because he had fallen in love with me and he was going to be ripped away from me. He then told me that he found out that he wasn't actually moving, and he asked if I could give him a second chance.

Jimmy: That seems like a justifiable reason to break up, even if it was a mean thing to do. How did you react?

Lila: I cussed him out. I told him that I had never loved him, that everything we had was a lie. I told him that he was an idiot for calling me up and to lose my number. [*Quieter*] He was sobbing when I hung up on him.

Jimmy: You were hurting.

Lila: Don't try to justify it! But there's more. Later that week I got called up about the musical. Someone had dropped out, and they wanted me for a part. I also got cast in a play at the same time. You know what I did?

Jimmy: Did the musical?

Lila: No! I turned down both parts, and I never did theater again.

Jimmy: Why would you do that?

Lila: Because I was sixteen and dramatic and very, very angry at the world. So angry that I ruined my life.

Jimmy: Lila—

Lila: Maybe I should just die. Maybe the world would be better if I didn't constantly put my hate and my anger and my awful emotions into the world.

Jimmy: Lila—

Lila: Oh Jimmy, I can't do this. I can't ever make up for what I've done. You only heard about that one time. There are so many more—

Jimmy: LILA.

Lila [*startled*]: What?

Jimmy: Just—just take a breath. Calm down. You're spiraling. [*He wipes a tear from her eye and takes her hand.*] Look at me. [*After she looks up at him, he continues.*] I have seen thousands of humans in my time, okay? They come from all different backgrounds, all different lives, all different times. I've had saints and demons. I've had people who chose to live, people who chose to die, people who couldn't choose and sat in their Wardrobes for centuries. But never—I repeat NEVER—have I seen someone who has truly ruined their life.

Lila: But—

Jimmy: Lila, you are not a failure. You are not a destroyer. You are human. Yes, sometimes a bad one, but human nonetheless. And as such, you can learn and grow from your mistakes. Tell me— did you ever break up with someone after Mark?

Lila [*sniffling*]: Yeah.

Jimmy: Were any of those breakups as bad as your first?

Lila: No.

Jimmy: That's because you learned and you grew. What did you do after theater?

Lila: I joined mathletes.

Jimmy: And what is your job now?

Lila: An accountant.

Jimmy: Yes, everything we do has consequences. Sometimes long-term, sometimes short-term. But you did not ruin your life. You just changed it. Tell me about what you were doing before you got hit by that car.

Lila: I was on my way to lunch with my boyfriend. He had gotten off work so that we could go to my favorite café.

Jimmy: And why were you hurrying so much that you didn't see the car?

Lila: Because I was going to pick up a present for him.

Jimmy: Describe the weather.

Lila: It was warm. The trees were all budded out in new growth, the birds were chirping, the cars were honking, yes, but in a nice way… wait a second. I thought that the reason I got run over was because I was angry?

Jimmy: No. You were having a good day. You were distracted because you were excited to see your boyfriend, and then you got hit. Simple as that.

Lila: I'm so confused.

Jimmy: I was confused too. I didn't understand why someone who had their life together and was relatively happy would be in a gray area. But then, after meeting L.E.… I unfortunately understood. As good as your life is, as good as you have it now, there's still that part of you that screams and cries like L.E. does. While you aren't mean to the world anymore—

Lila: I'm still mean to myself.

Jimmy: Bingo.

Lila: Oh, I—[*She's so overwhelmed that she bursts into tears. Jimmy pulls her into a hug, and they stay like that while he comforts her.*]

Lila [*muffled*]: I'm so sorry. I don't know why I'm acting like this.

Jimmy: You've never been to therapy, have you?

Lila: No.

Jimmy: You should try that. If you go back to your life, that is.

Lila: If I go back, how do I fix this mess? [*She gestures to herself.*]

Jimmy: People work on themselves lots of ways. Some exercise. Some pray. Some journal. But all of them realize that they have to forgive themselves, and I think that that is where you should start. But, of course, you don't have to go back.

[*Lila pulls away suddenly.*]

Lila: What do you mean, I don't have to go back? Of course I do! There is so much I have left to do, so many things I need to experience.

Jimmy [*holding back a smile*]: Are you sure?

Lila [*taking Jimmy's hands*]: I need to set this right. I need to learn to love myself like I love everyone else. My life is good, and I'll be okay. Please let me go back.

Jimmy: My wish is your command, my friend.

[*Jimmy snaps his fingers, and there's a blackout. Lights slowly fade up on Jimmy, who is sitting in the wooden chair, legs crossed, seemly content and deep in thought. He smiles as he hears a voice from offstage.*]

Old Lila [*offstage*]: Jimmy! My friend, how I've missed you!

[*Old Lila hobbles onto stage. She's smiling, wider than we've ever seen. Jimmy stands, and she rushes into his arms.*]

Old Lila: Thank you.

Jimmy: I take it that you enjoyed yourself?

Old Lila: It was wonderful, Jimmy, simply wonderful. I can't wait to tell you all about it. I've missed you so.

Jimmy: I take it that you're ready to move on to the next stage then, yes?

Old Lila: Will you be able to come with me?

Jimmy: Yes ma'am. [*He gives a salute, and she playfully slaps his arm.*] Is that a ring I see on your finger?

Old Lila [*showing it off*]: Isn't it lovely? We've been married for sixty-two years. He was planning on proposing to me at the café, but instead kneeled down next to my hospital bed. He's such a darling. [*She gives an excited gasp.*] He passed away last year. Will I get to see him now?

Jimmy: He's waiting for you on the other side.

Old Lila: Well then, let's go! I've told him all about you. I think you two will get along great. [*She pauses and looks up at him.*] Thank you, again.

Jimmy: For what?

Old Lila: For not giving up on me.

Jimmy: I was just doing my job.

Old Lila: Well, thank you for doing it well.

[*They smile at each other.*]

Jimmy: Now, what else happened while you were away?

[*As Old Lila starts chatting, Jimmy takes her by the arm and leads her offstage (the opposite side to the side that everyone entered on). Lights dim until blackout hits as they reach the wings.*]

THE END

SUBCONSCIOUS EXPLORATIONS

UVULA: A LOVE STORY

M.K. BRAKE   MOUNT HERMON, MA, US

You must find the belltower in the center of the city—you know this, though you do not know how—hover above you, see yourself as a child by a city—though you don't know how. Don't know how you can know you, spread as atmosphere or thought; how you are orbing, undulating, around a city that is you and that contains you—as you watch you—as you shield you from the sunray that must somehow exist outside all of you, because the city and the you by the city feel it on bare shoulders.

You watch yourself wind around the train tracks at the edge of the sienna city. You are wondering how the buildings in the distance are made of gray jelly. Perhaps it is that the atmosphere of you permeates them, that the city is in thrall of you, dense in the fog of you, ready to warp for you, so this, then, is how the city can part for the very *ness* of you, the child, the youth-you, onto whom you bend the beam of physics, and so guiding, let this place buckle like a parting of summer grass through which the youth-you can peacefully through. You let yourself be tantalized by the way a world parts. Look at the wonder of you, in cheek, how the suggestion of grass brushes your child face. Beckoned by the city, by this that you bent and built for beckoning—this which might be yourself.

At the gateway of the city, the bricks are orange under foot and people flicker in and out of doorways, and a woman—she's wearing a full skirt outside of time—might look at you as she hands another her basket, and she might squint at you in this handing as if to question physics—the physics of you—how are you *here*—before the answer to her question blinks her out of existence. It is the same with her gray-haired companion, though just before, they had been looking jovial. Then a stray dog bounds through where, just one moment ago, his masterless had paused in question, so it follows that whatever scent he follows is of his own devising. And because you are you and also all that which is contained in the world of you/that which protects the world of you, you know his path is just and to follow him.

The orange bricks, agitated, shake your feet and bloom. They gutter like desperate fireworks beneath you and fly forward, unfoot you as they form into sudden stacks now pluming in front of you. The dog saunters through the new door in the new tower that smokes its stacks, and you follow him inside, and when you walk inside, you are outside in a cornfield and the dog is gone and someone is waiting for you behind the wheel of a tractor, and the scene stiffens at sight, how husks stiffen in heat.

How is it that you know they are the one with the light eyes and the light hair who grew up neighborly in your never-home? The meeting of hands here implies a past—fingertips fervent above chores, butter-churning, alchemized by novelty—until one day, displaced by enigma, you landed here alone in the big orange city with the big eye of sky, and the refractions of light through your clouded sclera blink like a message behind a blimp: *'go to that body so you can know the body, for when you grow out of and past this. for the future.'*

You pass over the oil patch on the parched ground beside the tractor and pause to wonder at the contracted rainbow, toying, in your pocket like a coin, with the impossibility of a singular face, so that yours in the oil slick refracts a bird's-eye, and the youth-you catches a glimpse of what your atmosphere knows: that the city is wide and long, and the belltower rests in the center, with no bell, no chime, no gong. You palm the puddle, reaching into and for, but mirage-like, it yields but black.

Your lifeline soiled, you fumble to mount the tractor, but someone has been waiting there, with a soft gray rag, to keep you. As you sidle up beside them on the black leather seat, they take your hand and wipe it clean, and your knowledge, overhead like a sun, watches and beams on— making the leather crackle and little thighs sweat, slipping in stature— two small bodies holding one another, lost in silence as the hard earth and the expanse of sky couple at horizon.

How you know you know someone is how you both recognize the coupling with no need to say it—*coupling*. There is a quake in the *ness/ nucleus* of you; the earth rumbles, and the buildings shake. This might be a question of the necessity of rupture. It might be when you and another fuse. Even you don't know if this is fissioning or fusing, but you do know recognition is a kind of knowledge once-removed, and you wonder: What iteration of you could know what exists outside the *ness* of knowing? Big bangs, new galaxies, undersides of souls. Someone lays feet upon your crusted soil, trekking towards your center, and so is in the world of you yet somehow a stranger still because they are not yet consumed at the core of you, whose warm gravity spins the need to know you and to know where it all went wandering.

How you acquiesce to question is cornfield dissolving to urbanity. Beyond the yellow field, up into the sky, the knobbled scape of city grasps. Swelling alongside steeples are space needles; a garden grows; blight blights. The dry heat knows, even as you cup their hand in yours, that you move towards the other's departure. And you do not need your most loaded know of world-building to know this: the other does not know—goodbye looming in premature gong. You look at them—cheeks just pixelations, eyes just prisms—and in so doing, conceive a threshold; the threshold between the introduction of agency and the commitment to act; this, the threshold where you wish it were not impossible to linger. This is the first and only instance you will divorce diorama-heart-of-you from matured-head-of-you, to dissent. Not to want to leave this moment. Or lie. Then, a second quake, a fear in the *ness* of you, warbling all the way to the ether of you, almost unseating you: that you will break from you, glitch downward into the gray matter of you, where you can forever contain this moment, somewhere, yet never locate it again. How something good becomes a splinter.

But that which contains all yous, which contains the quaking, knows better. Hands clasped together, it can be easy to be lulled by the clean scent of covalence on the air. But the most alluring of all knows is the un-known; the always-future-know; the as-yet-to-be-fulfilled. The know you do not yet know but know you will one day know that will be the changes in you. When ease, transmuted to need, allows you to choose to give or receive. How the greatest of bonds arise from will. So you lead the other (though you wish to journey *with* the other, you know you lead the other) into the deserted city. Sliding from the tractor, your feet touch down in an absent city square. You are just slightly alarmed. The people do not even flicker now, exist only as a thrum of specters, like if radio static had a shadow, if thunder were a shape and not a sound.

Your wish for cicada brings you to the belltower, wherein silence is weld of cogless and metal scraps shaved from the making of bolts. You know that when the other enters, they must do so alone, know what you don't know, the need for utterance, but youth-you stagnates on the brink of a question: how the city erected this thrall of sound, this belltower, this uvula fossilized.

But inside the monument, you know, is the world of trembles. Inside, you are a word of trembles. The trembling *ness* at the core of you wonders at the scope of your iterations. How moved are you? What is the 777-times-removed-you? If the palm of you—the lifeline-soiled-train-track-giving-way-to-prairie-grass—holds a psalm for you? How, inside this all-of-you, another might be a key, i.e., the silent town would be so much richer with the ringing of bells.

You want to say now, '*they smile*', but the other is not yet aware they move to enter the uvula, which is the belltower unbricking an other-sized gape for a door, its newly minted edges glowing ember. They let you let go of their hand to let them into you. They walk three steps. They don't look back. They pause at the threshold, readying to unleash what lies within.

For the world may be sick. Not with disease or famine, no, but something subtle, insidious, seemingly cemented to the very structure of this plane, its very system of being. You felt not nauseous before but will have the all-of-you unfurl for you, how only a tongue can, to check to be sure. At your signal, with tongue-depressor, elbow grease, the other wrenches the door: say ahh, open wider, say...

Ahhhhhhhhhhhh.

Now this world is a world engulfed in flood. Now this: a sound bath of epic proportions. Regurgitation. Regenesis. The outward pouring of all of everything inside, and when someone nestles inside, something inside you settles. Forty days and forty nights; salt water and Betadine; gargling to the sky and sighing north. How the dead nature of a star does not compromise its beauty is how your world is swallowed without pain. When the uvula ungags and to ask is to act.

ABOUT THE WRITERS

This collection of interpretations of the confidence theme was created with imagination and flair by the winning and commended writers from the Minds Shine Bright Writing Competition, announced in early 2024.

DEE BARRAGRY is an Irish writer, photographer and artist. A childhood spent between Ireland, Saudi Arabia and Mexico ignited an innate curiosity about origins, identity, and legacy. *The Lampwick Chronicles*, her debut children's novel, will be published by Walker Books in 2025.

CIARA BLUM is a medical student who has, perhaps unexpectedly, always had a keen interest in creative writing. Her short story 'Realer Than Real' explores a young child's battle with altering perceptions of reality. A near-death experience grants him a new outlook on, and understanding of, the world around him and how he exists in it.

HELEN BOOTH lives on beautiful Wadawurrung Country and loves reading, learning about, and writing short fiction. Her stories have made longlists and shortlists for several prizes, and she won the 2022 Apollo Bay WORDfest and 2018 Odyssey House short story prizes.

M.K. BRAKE is a writer from Southeastern United States. She holds an MFA in Poetry from Louisiana State University and an MFA in Nonfiction from the Nonfiction Writing Program at the University of Iowa. Her debut chapbook, *The Taxidermist's Girl*, was published in 2016 by dancing girl press and her work can be found in *Bone Bouquet*, *Bayou Magazine*, Wesleyan University's *Best American Experimental Writing*, and others. She currently lives with her partner and kiddo in the Berkshires.

HANNAH BROWN grew up exploring the rocks and crags of Welsh beaches and has since graduated to living amongst the islands of Tokyo Bay. By day, she teaches writing to teenagers, and by night, she writes until she drops. You can find her on X @Hannah_Aimee_17.

JONATHAN CHIBUIKE UKAH is a Pushcart Prize-nominated poet living in the United Kingdom. His poems have been featured in *Atticus Review*, *The Pierian*, *Unleash Lit*, *Impostor*, *The Journal of Undiscovered Poets*, and elsewhere. He is a winner of the 2022 Voices of Lincoln Poetry Contest and the 2023 Alexander Pope Award. He was also a second runner-up in the Wingless Dreamer poetry prize in 2023.

HELEN DOSEDEL is a senior at Mound Westonka High School, Minnesota. She plans to attend college in the fall, majoring in English literature and minoring in creative writing. In the meantime, she spends her time writing, reading and learning.

MOLLY DUNN is a Year 11 student at Mansfield Secondary College and has had a passion for reading and writing from a very young age. Last year, she was longlisted and published in the Mansfield Readers and Writers national short story competition for her story 'Held by the Sea', and this year, was shortlisted in the same competition with her story 'Small Town God'.

LEONE GABRIELLE writes from Seymour, a snaking river town in Central Victoria on Taungurung country. She has been published in *Cordite Poetry Review*, *Australian Poetry*, *Pure Slush*, *Plumwood Mountain*, *Mona Magazine*, *MASKS Literary Magazine*, *XR Global*, *Meanjin Quarterly*, *Minds Shine Bright*, *Spineless Wonders*, *Rochford Street Review*. When not writing, she is in the company of snails and goldfish.

Born and raised in Edmonton, AB, Canada, SHARMAINE GRAY is a child of the prairies, a descendant of the Cree, French, Scottish, Irish and Iroquois. Linguistically gifted, Sharmaine's father taught her the love of words, which inspired her to start writing poetry at the age of eleven and to eventually learn French.

JONATHAN GREENHAUSE's first poetry collection, *Cupping Our Palms* (Meadowlark Press, 2022), was the winner of the 2022 Birdy Poetry Prize, and his poems have appeared or are forthcoming in *Antithesis*, *The Ginkgo Prize for Ecopoetry*, *Going Down Swinging*, *LitMag*, *Poetry Ireland Review*, and *The Poetry Society* website.

JENNIFER LEIGH HARRISON is a poet and painter living in Seattle. She was the recipient of the Marian Coe Scholarship in creative writing. Her poems have most recently appeared in *Eastern Iowa Review*, *Cathexis Northwest Press*, *Ubu*, and elsewhere. She is the author of the chapbook *Places We Left*, published by dancing girl press.

When not creating art or writing poetry, SUSAN Y. HOFFMAN spends time tutoring, gardening, and promoting literacy through her blog: susanyounghoffman.wordpress.com. While on long walks, she is a keen observer of human interactions with nature, which inspire her writing. Her artwork in acrylic and watercolor ranges from abstract art, to realistic portraits, and landscapes.

MAILE JUAREZ spent her childhood traveling the US as a military kid and her short stint of adulthood traveling the world. She's been obsessed with writing since she was a young child, and her stories have always been inspired by the amazing people and places she's seen. Her dream is to be a published novelist with a vegetable garden.

NIAMH KELLEHER is a seventeen-year-old aspiring author. Her entry is closely connected to her personal experiences of being in hospital for surgeries, drawing upon from her real emotions. Niamh aimed to communicate the theme of fostering confidence and hope, and in particular,highlighting the amazing strength of those who face hardships yet still have a smile on their face and hope in their heart.

GRACE KELLER is a playwright and fiction writer from Dallas, Texas. She is currently pursuing a Bachelor of Arts from Trinity University. A storyteller from birth, she hopes that her writing will one day make a difference in the world. In her spare time, Grace enjoys acting, crocheting, and playing with her cats, Heady and Kiwi.

ZOFIA KUYPERS lives in Sydney's Eastern Suburbs with her husband, two young children and poodle. An engineer by training, Zofia spends her days with her family, volunteering at her children's school, and writing.

KATHRYN LE MON earned her BA from Kenyon College and is presently an MFA candidate at The Ohio State University where she serves as the Production and Online Editor for *The Journal*. She is the winner of *Flash Frog*'s 2023 The Blue Frog award in flash fiction. Her work has appeared in *Flash Frog*, *After Dinner Conversation*, *Gigantic Sequins*, and elsewhere.

CAITLIN MAHONY lives in Bacchus Marsh, Victoria, Australia. She won the Port Stephens Literature Award 2023, was highly commended in the Peter Cowan Short Story Competition 2023, and is in the AWC Furious Fiction showcase for October 2023 and *The Suburban Review's Hills Hoist Volume 3*. Caitlin's work draws inspiration from nature, humanity, and the realities of living with chronic illness.

KATY MASSEY is quite new to writing short stories. She was a journalist in the UK for many years before studying for an MA and PhD in Creative Writing. Her memoir, *Are We Home Yet?*, was published in 2020, praised by Bernardine Evaristo as 'a gem', and shortlisted for the Jhalak Prize and Portico Prize. Her first novel, *All Us Sinners*, was recently published by Sphere.

ANDREA McMAHON's stories have been published in journals and collections, including *Island* and *Forty South*. Her story 'The Cuckoo's Nest' won the 2023 Lane Cove Short Story Prize; and 'Damselfly', the 2020 Tasmanian Writers' Prize. Andrea lives in Hobart and has worked as a librarian and library adult literacy practitioner. More of Andrea's writing can be found at andreaswriting.wordpress.com.

DAN MICKLETHWAITE writes stories in the north of England, some of which have featured in *The Dread Machine*, *IZ Digital*, and *NewMyths*. His debut novel, *The Less Than Perfect Legend of Donna Creosote*, was published by Bluemoose Books. He is currently working on his second novel. In his free time, he enjoys bouldering, both indoors and out.
Bio photo by J Micklethwaite.

TAMRA PALMER is a seasoned writer, having worked on Australian and international children's television programs; an article writer for national magazines and publications, she has also had several short stories and poems published. She now has a middle grade novel and an adult novel in development.

SUE PINCHAM mostly writes short fiction and has had her work published in numerous anthologies. She lives near the beach on the NSW South Coast.

MATTHEW PITT operates out of Fort Worth, Texas, as an Associate Professor of Creative Writing at TCU. Pitt's third book, *The Be-everything! Brothers* (a novella), is forthcoming later this year. His stories have won numerous awards and pats, and appear in *Story*, *Michigan Quarterly Review*, *BOMB*, *EPOCH*, *Oxford American*, *Blackbird*, The *Cincinnati Review*, *Conjunctions*, and *The Southern Review*. Matt's recent fiction was longlisted for the Elizabeth Jolley Prize, coordinated by the *Australian Book Review*. *Bio photo by Leo Wesson.*

Fueled by the delightfully absurd, RYLAN RAFFERTY treasures tales of whimsy and monsters. Her writing accolades include finalist placements in ScreenCraft's Comedy Screenplay Competition, Fresh Voices Screenplay Competition and Barnstorm Fest. Her two short horror films have screened at various festivals. Rylan continues to pursue her passion for storytelling in Los Angeles as a film editor, writer, and director, with her two furry assistants, Graybe and Colors.

MAX RIDDINGTON works in PR and journalism. Writing helps her through the best-&-worst-&-Netflix-is-down times. She'd be lost without both.

EMILY ROBERTSON is an emerging author from Pinjarra, Western Australia. When she is not studying creative writing at Curtin University, she is busy raising her two boys *and* her husband.

SHOSHANNA ROCKMAN is a multi-award winning writer, editor and performance poet. She has been widely published nationally and internationally. Her poems have appeared in *The Canberra Times*, *Cordite Poetry Review*, *Antipodes*, *Confidence Minds Shine Bright Anthology 2022*, and many more.

F.L. ROSE is a novelist, short story writer and poet, living on a rural property on the beautiful south-east coast of Australia. As an author, she's drawn to the dark side of human experience, experimenting with horror, gothic overkill and the literary thriller, but in daily life, she's absorbed by pruning issues, tomato growing and dogs. You can find out more about F.L. Rose on her author website at www.fallaciousrose.com.

A German translator by trade, EVI RUHLE initially began writing short stories to maintain and refine her English skills. She went on to study several units of creative writing, and two of her stories have been published by Swamp. Currently, she is working on a novel. Evi has lived in London, Berlin and Melbourne, and her writing is inspired by these places.

JOSIANE SMITH writes regularly for the international press on arts and spirituality in social change. She is co-editor for *Magma*'s 89th issue on 'performance' and the incoming Chair of the Quaker Arts Network. Her poems have featured in online and print publications, including Minds Shine Bright (Australia) and the Mindful Poetry Moments (USA) anthologies, as well as in arts exhibitions in Cape Town, Amman, Beirut and the USA. She is writing a non-fiction book on the 'Zeitgeist'.

ALICIA SOMETIMES is a writer and broadcaster. She has performed her spoken word and poetry at many venues, festivals and events around the world. Her poems have been in *The Best Australian Science Writing*, *The Best Australian Poems*, and many more. In 2023, she received an ANAT Synapse artist residency and co-created an art installation for Science Gallery Melbourne's exhibition, DARK MATTERS.

CATALINA STERIU has a Bachelor's degree in literary arts from the University of Bucharest and is passionate about reading and writing. She made her authorial debut in Belgium in 2020, after winning a short story contest. The same year, she won another four literary competitions in Paris and was published each time in collective volumes. She also won two national literary prizes in Romania, and in 2023 she published a short stories volume.

BOB TOPPING lives in rural, south-eastern Queensland. Many of his short stories have been shortlisted and published. He is inspired by eccentric characters in diverse settings in this wide and wonderful country.

KYM TYZACK grew up in Geelong and now lives on the Bellarine Peninsula. She has worked as a secondary school English and history teacher, a library officer, and as a further education coordinator. As well as writing short stories, Kym is working on a young adult novel. Her story, 'Leaving', was published in *The Furphy Anthology 2022*.

VALERIE WALLACE is the author of *House of McQueen*, selected by Vievee Francis for the Four Way Books Intro Prize in Poetry, and named one of the best books of the year by the Chicago Review of Books. Her work appears in *Poetry*, poets.org, *The Eloquent Poem*, and more. Learn more about her work at valeriewallace.net.

JAZ WARD, now beginning her twenties, finds solace and inspiration in the realms of literature and writing. For her, these pursuits serve as a means to either escape from the imminent reality of her adulthood, or, at times, wholeheartedly embrace it. In discovering this comfort in the written word, Jaz is studying to become an English teacher, so that this love of literature can be shared.

PAUL WEIDKNECHT is the author of *Native to This Stream: Brief Writings About Fly-Fishing & the Great Outdoors*, a chapbook collection of previously published short stories, essays, and poems. He wrote the short film *Know Thy Partner*, and his work has appeared in *Gray's Sporting Journal*, *Outdoor Life*, *Rosebud*, *Shenandoah*, *Structo* (UK), and elsewhere. He is currently editing his feature-length screenplay on the first African-American war hero.

STEPHANIE WILLIAMS-HOLMES is an English
Literature student from Christchurch, New Zealand,
who loves writing poetry and flash fiction that
explores the body and mind through metaphor. 'Self-
Portrait' explores self-image and how searching for
validation from social media to boost our confidence
can, and often does, backfire.